DEMCO

the
Heart
Reader

the Heart Reader

Anonymous

WORD PUBLISHING

NASHVILLE

A Thomas Nelson Company

ISBN 0-7394-1060-1

At this, the man's ears were opened, his tongue was loosened and he began to speak plainly.

MARK 7:35

1

The dream came on a Sunday night, after an afternoon of golf and an evening of watching politicians debate on cable. Like some divine hand, it seemed to grab Sam Bennett by the collar and pull him under. As if he were trapped in front of a huge movie screen, he saw a woman in a tiny room with a tin roof and a dirt floor, searching desperately for something. She grabbed things down from cupboards, off of shelves, turned things over, removed the cushions from her couch, searched behind doors and under rugs. It was a frustrating dream, one that seemed to have no end, until finally, Sam saw a coin, carelessly dropped in the corner of the room. The woman in the dream saw it at the same time, and she fell on it and snatched it up and began to weep with joy.

One lousy coin? he thought. *Why would she be so excited over one lousy coin?* Restlessly, Sam turned over in his sleep and buried his face in his pillow. The words of his pastor's sermon earlier that day played over and over in his mind. Words about reaching a hurting world. About hearing people's spiritual needs. He hadn't even listened that hard when the preacher had uttered them, but now they came back to him like recorded phrases that reeled around and around and around in his head, refusing to leave him until they sank in.

And then he heard the voice, the voice that woke him as it reverberated through his mind with holy power. "Ephphatha! Ephphatha!" He sat upright in bed.

The word vibrated through him, though he didn't know its meaning. It was Hebrew, he thought. Or, perhaps, Greek. And whose was the voice?

He was wide awake now, drenched in a cold sweat, and he was trembling. Kate, his wife, lay next to him, undisturbed. Quietly, he got out of bed and stumbled through the house. He went to the kitchen sink and splashed water on his face, then headed for the comfort and refuge of his recliner. It was four o'clock in the morning, too early to be up, yet he couldn't go back to sleep. It wasn't the dream that disturbed him so much, but the voice. It had had such power, such authority.

Ephphatha! What did it mean? Now that he thought of it, he was sure the voice hadn't been a part of the dream. He had only seen the woman, the coin in his sleep. No, the voice had the authority of God. Could the Lord have spoken to him tonight? But why would he speak in another language? Why would God utter something that so disturbed his spirit, something resonating with importance, but something he wasn't able to understand? Was it some kind of sign, or was he just losing it?

He took a deep breath and tried to shake the cobwebs out of his brain. The thought of going back to bed and facing more of the same was out of the question, so he finally put on a pot of coffee. After it had brewed, he poured a cup, then sat there sipping on it, trying to decide if the dream was something he should give more thought, or if he should dismiss it altogether.

Did it have something to do with the sermon he had yawned through yesterday? John, the pastor, had been waxing eloquent about the lost sheep. Something about leaving ninety-nine to go after one.

Sam had been more interested in the second hand on his watch. He'd figured if John didn't wind down soon, there would be a ridiculous line at every restaurant in town.

Was that why he'd had the dream? Did that word, *Ephphatha*, contain some kind of rebuke about listening in church? Now that he thought about it, John had been on a roll yesterday. By the end of the sermon, his face was reddening and he was leaning over the pulpit, shaking his hands to make his point. Sam hadn't seen John that worked up since he'd given his life to ministry during their sophomore year of college. Back then, John had often gotten red-faced and loud when he tried to change the hearts of Sam and his friends. Sam had hoped it wouldn't mean that John would give a long, drawn-out benediction, then have them sing all four verses of the final hymn, while the Presbyterians got to the restaurants first.

"Have you ever considered what God hears in the hearts of people?" the pastor had asked. "What spiritual needs cry out to him? What if we could hear with God's ears?" Then he had looked around the sanctuary at the faces one by one. His eyes had met Sam's, and Sam tried to look more awake. He felt guilty when he saw disappointment cross over John's face.

"Most of you don't even hear with the ears you have," the pastor said in a duller voice. "Your ears are clogged up, and you can't hear the most obvious things. So there are people with needs out there just crying to be met, yet so few of God's laborers are going out to rescue them. If you want to hear, if you want to truly see, come to the altar now. Get on your knees and ask God to use you."

If God was mad at him now, Sam thought, it was because of his attitude yesterday. Sam had checked his watch again. He remembered thinking that if anyone went to that altar during the first verse and ripped out a quick prayer of commitment, they might still get out of there by twelve. If no one came, they might wind down after the second verse. But after the second verse, the pastor had nodded to the choir director to keep the song going. He said that he knew there was someone out there who felt the Holy Spirit calling, and he didn't want to close the service until they did their business with God.

Sam had actually considered going himself, just to wrap things up.

When no one responded, the pastor finally gave up and brought the service to an end. Sam hadn't wasted any time grabbing his wife's hand, making his way out of the pew, and pushing through the crowd to the exit door. He hadn't given the sermon another thought.

Now he tried to sort back through the points in that sermon. Was there something there about lost coins? Had John mentioned that unknown word? Had all of it somehow gotten snagged in his consciousness, even though he couldn't remember it now?

He was still trying to understand the dream when Kate got up some time later. "You're up early," she said.

He sipped his coffee. "Couldn't sleep."

"Was I stealing the covers?"

"No. I just had some dreams."

"Bad ones?"

He shrugged. "No, not really. Just weird stuff. You know the kind. Something's lost and you can't find it."

"I have those dreams," Kate said, her sleepy eyes widening. "I'm running through the airport to catch a plane, but I can't seem to make the gate. Or I'm in college and I'm trying to get to my final exam, only I haven't been to class all semester and don't know where the room is. Or I have to speak to a room full of people, and I look down and realize I'm still in my pajamas—"

"It wasn't like that," he cut in, irritated. "It was a little scarier."

"Scary? Why?"

He frowned. "I don't know. I'm not sure."

She considered that for a moment. "I have scary dreams sometimes too. The ones where someone's about to hurt me, but I can't scream." She poured herself a cup of coffee, then remembered another one. "Or the one where someone's throwing matches at me, but I can't put them out . . ."

He gazed at his wife. "Kate, have you thought of getting psychiatric help?"

"Hey, you're the one who couldn't sleep last night. I slept like a baby." She brought the cup to her lips.

"I want to be useful."

He frowned at the out-of-context comment, then decided that she meant it in regard to his dreams. "Don't worry about me." He got up and stretched. "Guess I'll go take my shower."

By the time he had showered and dressed, he was feeling a little better. The dream was just a dream, he thought, just a collage of images and phrases that he'd heard in the last few days. The preacher's message, something they'd talked about in Sunday school, maybe something he'd overheard subconsciously. It didn't matter. It had all mixed together in some kind of virus of thoughts, and his brain was just coughing it up as he slept. There was nothing to worry about.

2

After he'd taken Kate to work at the hospital, he parked in front of the diner across the street. Kate wasn't a breakfast eater, but he liked the works. Years ago, when they still had children at home, they had settled into a routine of drinking coffee together in the mornings, then going their separate ways. Now, when she headed for the hospital at seven, he headed for the diner to eat breakfast.

Still a little more unsettled than he wanted to admit, he went into the diner and took a seat at the counter. The popular place was loud with barely controlled chaos that always got his adrenaline pumping. In the front, irritable waitresses yelled orders to each other, and occasionally Sam could hear Leon, the cook in the back, let out a stream of curses that made Sam consider swearing the place off. But he always came back. Nowhere else could he get his eggs cooked exactly right.

He picked up the newspaper someone had left on the counter and scanned the headlines. Janie, his regular waitress, looked distracted as she approached him. "Morning, Sam. You're a little early today."

"Yeah," he muttered without looking up, "I had trouble sleeping."

"A little rest could change my whole life."

Now he looked up at her. She looked tired and had circles under her eyes and wrinkles he hadn't noticed before. He wondered how old she was. Forty? Forty-five? "Yeah? You can't sleep, either?" he asked.

She frowned and gazed across the counter. "Huh?"

"What you said about rest."

Her eyes narrowed. "Sam, all I said is that you're here early this morning. You sure you're all right?"

He stared at her for a moment. Hadn't he heard her say something about rest? He shook his head. "Whatever. I'll take the usual."

He watched, perplexed, as she went to yell his order to the angry cook.

The voice of the woman sitting two stools down from him distracted him from Janie. "Gravity's just gonna let go of me, and I'm gonna go flying out into the universe."

Amused, Sam glanced over at her. "That's a new variation on the 'stop the world I want to get off' theme."

Startled, the woman looked up at him. "What is?"

His grin faded. "I'm sorry. I thought you were talking to me."

She touched her hair with a shaky hand. "I didn't say anything."

"Oh," he said, "sorry." He forced himself to look back down at the newspaper. After a second, he heard the voice again.

"I'm gonna hurl out into the universe and no one will notice I'm gone." He looked at the woman again. She had tears in her eyes, and he knew without a doubt that the hopeless words had come from her.

He cleared his throat and leaned toward her. "That time . . . were you talking to me?"

She looked annoyed. "I wasn't talking to anyone. I'm just sitting here minding my own business."

He was getting aggravated. Who was she trying to kid? He was positive he'd heard her. "You didn't *say* anything?"

"No!"

Janie came back with his breakfast just as the woman belted out the denial. "Sam, you're not causing trouble with our other customers, are you?" she asked with a wink.

He shook his head. The woman was giving him the creeps. "I must be hearing things. Look, I think I'll go sit at that table."

Janie nodded, so he stuffed the paper under his arm, grabbed his plate and coffee, and moved over to the empty booth in the corner. He set his coffee down and slipped into his seat and began to eat. The place was filling up with nurses and medical students from the hospital across the street. Normally, he saw the same faces every day, but he rarely spoke to any of them.

"There's just no point," the man at the table next to him said.

Sam looked over his shoulder. "In what?"

The man shot him a look. "Excuse me?"

"You said there's just no point. In what?"

The man looked shaken. "Uh . . . I must have been thinking out loud. Guess I'm farther gone than I thought. Sorry."

"It's okay," Sam said. "No biggie." He started to eat but the man spoke again.

"If I could just have more than a ten minute conversation . . . have somebody really listen . . . be heard . . ."

Sam looked up again, starting to get angry. What was this guy's problem? Why did he insist on pouring his heart out to Sam? But the man wasn't looking at him—he was staring down at his plate. The words were still coming, but his mouth wasn't moving.

"Everybody's always in a hurry. Nobody has time."

Slowly, Sam began to realize that the man wasn't speaking. Neither had the woman or Janie . . . He wasn't hearing audible words or voices, although they sure sounded that way to him.

He sat back hard in his booth. What was happening to him? He knew he wasn't still dreaming. He was wide awake—the coffee even burned his tongue. Everything was normal, except for those voices.

Abandoning his plate, he rushed out of the diner and headed back to his car. A woman with a long red braid was standing near it, waiting to cross the street. His hands trembled as he sorted through his key chain for the key to open his car door.

"I am my past," the woman said.

He turned around. Once again, he realized she hadn't spoken the words aloud.

"I'll always be what he turned me into. I'll never escape it."

He stood there for a moment, stunned, listening to the voice that seemed to come from nowhere. He saw tears glistening in her eyes as she watched the cars whiz by, and he knew that what he'd heard was something inside her—deep down.

Was he losing his mind?

"*Abuse* is such a clean, sterile word," she went on, and he realized that the preoccupation she seemed to have with waiting for a break in the traffic was really the despair she thought no one could hear.

She glanced his way, and he thought of approaching her, saying something like, *Your past hasn't set your future. There's Jesus Christ. He can change everything.*

But instead, he panicked and got into his car. What if he botched it up? What if she looked at him as one of those Bible-thumping fanatics who went around shoving their beliefs down people's throats? What if he made himself look stupid? Or worse, crazy?

Finally, she crossed the street, hurrying between cars, no longer waiting for a break in the traffic. He heard tires screech and a cab driver cursing, but the woman vanished into the crowd on the sidewalk. Sam sat frozen behind the wheel, marveling at her lack of regard for life . . . or death. The next time she crossed the street, would her desperation plunge her into even greater danger? Would her death wish be granted?

And how had he heard her desperate thoughts?

He sat, paralyzed, behind the wheel. His head was beginning to ache, and tears filled his eyes. His hands were trembling too badly to get the key into the ignition.

He looked at the clock. It was time for him to head for work. If he could just get behind his desk and bury himself in business, he could forget this bizarre morning.

Finally managing to start the car, he pulled out into the traffic and drove the three blocks over to his office building. He turned into the parking garage and found his own space with the sign that read "Sam Bennett, VP, Simpson Advertising." He got out and breathed in the crisp morning air, hoping it would cleanse his brain of this insanity and enable him to function.

He got onto the elevator and spoke to Jimmy, a young man with Down's Syndrome who ran the elevator nine hours a day. "Hi, Jimmy," he said.

"Hi, Mitter Bennett. How are you today?"

He looked down at the floor, waiting for Jimmy to push the button. "Fine. Just fine." As they rose to the thirteenth floor, he heard Jimmy's voice again.

"Wish I's a real person."

He looked up and saw that Jimmy was sitting on the stool, staring at the numbers as they changed. Sam's heart ached at the simple words he had heard. "Jimmy?" he asked.

"Yes sir, Mitter Bennett," the young man said.

"You are a real person."

"Yes sir, Mitter Bennett."

Confused, and not certain now whether he'd really heard Jimmy or not, Sam stumbled out when the doors opened. Behind him, Jimmy called, "Have a good day, Mitter Bennett."

Sam nodded and gave him a cursory wave, then headed for his office. He passed his secretary on the way in.

"Mornin', Sam," she said. "How's it going?"

"Good, Sally. Any messages so far?"

"Not yet."

He stood at her desk and scanned her calendar to see what was on his agenda today. She pulled her chair up and began jotting his appointments on a separate sheet of paper.

"Eleven, six, fifty-seven."

He glanced at her and saw that she was busy writing. "What was that?" he asked.

She looked up at him, perplexed. "What?"

"Didn't you say something?" He was sweating now. His tie felt too tight; it was constricting his breath.

"I said no messages."

"No! After that."

Slowly, she got up. "Sam, are you sure you're all right? You're looking a little pale."

"I'm fine," he snapped. "Maybe I need a glass of water."

"I'll get you one."

As she headed quickly for the lounge, Sam went into his office and sat down. Things were getting too weird. Nothing made any sense. Sally brought him the water, and he gulped it down, but it didn't do much to help him.

"Do you have a fever?" she asked, touching his forehead maternally.

"No, I just didn't sleep very well last night. I keep thinking I'm hearing people talking." He frowned, realizing what she must be thinking. He was delusional. But he didn't hear any such thought from her. Instead, she repeated, "Eleven, six, fifty-seven . . . It has to win. It has to."

Sam sucked in a breath. "A lottery ticket?" he asked.

The question startled her. She looked as though she'd just gotten caught stealing. "I didn't—"

"No, don't defend yourself," he said, getting up. "I don't care. I just want to know. Are you trying to win the lottery?"

She looked embarrassed for a moment, then after a few seconds, compressed her lips and threw her chin up. "Yes, Sam, I am. You see, I don't make the kind of money you make, so I have to take other opportunities."

"The numbers," he said. "Were they eleven, six, fifty-seven?"

Her gasp could have sucked in an insect from the other side of town. "I knew it!" she shouted. "They're winning numbers. First I heard them on the radio. This guy had kids ages eleven and six, and it was fifty-seven degrees when I got up. And those are the numbers of my birthday! And there were eleven red lights on the way to work and six stop signs, and I saw a flock of birds that must have had fifty-seven—"

He moaned and dropped back down. "Sally, this is a stretch. You're looking for those numbers, but the chances of your winning—"

"Then how come you just spouted them out to me? It's affirmation, Sam! If I wasn't sure before, I am now! The Lord gave me these numbers!"

"Sally, the Lord does a lot of things, but I don't think he picks lottery numbers. My understanding is that he isn't big on gambling."

"Well, you just wait and see," she said.

"If I win, he'll see what I'm worth." This time her lips didn't move.

There it was again. One of those thoughts. He wiped the sweat from his forehead and covered his ears.

"You don't look so good, Sam," she said. "Maybe I should call Kate. She could get you in to see a doctor."

"I don't need a doctor. It's these stupid voices!"

"I had a friend once who kept hearing voices, and it turned out she was picking up radio waves on her fillings. You don't have any new fillings, do you?"

"It's not the radio. It's . . . real voices." He was making no sense at all. This was madness. These voices obviously weren't real, or he would see the mouths move. Maybe he was still dreaming. Maybe he just needed to wake up.

But it didn't feel like a dream.

He got to his feet. "You know, come to think of it, maybe I do need a doctor." He ran his shaking hands through his hair. "Uh . . .

look, cover for me for a couple of hours, will you? I need to get out of here, get some fresh air."

"Sure thing, Sam. Your first appointment isn't until eleven, so don't worry about it."

He practically ran up the hall to get away, but he changed his mind before he got to the elevator. He didn't want to be on it with Jimmy again, so he took the stairwell and ran all thirteen floors down. He was perspiring and out of breath when he got to his car. He just needed some Tylenol, he thought. He needed to go to the closest store and get some medicine to help him.

There was a supermarket a mile up the street, so he drove there as fast as he could, almost running over a pedestrian as he turned into the parking lot. He pulled into handicap parking and sat there for a moment, feeling as disabled as anyone who couldn't walk. Finally, he got out and headed in.

He had never been to this store before, so he didn't know where the Tylenol would be. He headed up aisle one and passed a woman standing with a jar of peanut butter in her hand. "We're gonna go hungry," he heard her say. "I can't provide."

He turned around and knew instantly she hadn't said it aloud. She gave him a startled glance and put the peanut butter back. He shrugged out of his coat and almost ran into a teenaged couple standing in front of the school supplies. They were discussing the size of index cards they needed, but as he passed, he heard two other simultaneous voices.

"The pressure . . . it's too much."

"I just want somebody to love me."

He bolted around the corner, and thankfully, came to the Tylenol. He grabbed at the first package he saw, knocking the rest off of the shelf. Trembling, he knelt down and began picking up the boxes. A woman who worked there came up and started helping him. "Are you all right, sir?"

"Yes . . . fine . . . just a little clumsy . . ." He got to his feet and tried to stack the boxes again.

"I'm nobody. He won't even look me in the eye," a voice said.

He told himself he wasn't hearing what he was hearing and took off up the aisle to the cash register. Standing there, his heart pounding, he waited for the man in front of him to pay.

"I miss my family. What have I done?" The man's mouth was set in a grim line as he sorted through his wallet.

Sam turned away and saw the woman with the peanut butter behind him. "They'll go to bed hungry again. I can't take care of myself, much less them."

He tried to open the Tylenol package, but his hand was shaking too badly. He heard the girl behind the cash register muttering, "This is as good as it gets."

Deciding that the Tylenol wasn't going to help anyway, he dropped it onto the belt, pushed past the man, and ran back out to his car.

He got in and locked the door and sat there for a moment, reveling in the silence. He didn't want to get out again. He couldn't take the chance of being around people, of hearing those voices.

He needed help, he thought. Someone to talk to. Someone to tell him what was happening to him. He thought of John, his pastor. John had always listened to him, even before Sam gave his life to Christ. He was a good listener. Nothing had shocked John, not even Sam's sinful past.

He pulled out of the parking lot, and driving as if his mental health depended on his speed, he headed for the church.

3

John was just pulling into the church parking lot when Sam drove up. It seemed late—midmorning at least. But as the pastor waved and got out of his car, Sam realized that it was not quite eight. None of the rest of the church staff had made it in yet.

He got out and leaned wearily against the hood as John came around his car. "Sam, are you all right?"

"No," he said. "No, I'm not. Can I talk to you in private?"

John looked around as if to say that they *were* in private, then said, "Sure. Let's go into my office."

Sam managed to hold his confusion in as John escorted him into the church and up the hall to his office. He hadn't been in John's office in a very long time, not since he'd helped paint the place three years before. He went in and slumped down in the chair across from John's desk.

John took the chair next to him and sat facing him. His elbows on his knees, he leaned forward in a gesture of concern. "Tell me, Sam. What's wrong?"

"I can hear things," Sam blurted. "Everywhere I go . . . I hear voices. Talking at me from every direction, every person I pass. I think I'm losing it!"

John sat straighter, letting the words sink in. "What kind of voices?"

Sam got up and went to the window, looked out, and raked his hand through his hair. "Just . . . voices. Like thoughts."

"Talking to you?"

"No, not me, really. It's like . . . it really doesn't have anything to do with me. I just overhear. Like I'm eavesdropping . . ."

He swung back around and saw the twisted expression on the pastor's face. He sounded like someone on drugs, Sam realized.

"Sam, how long have you been this way?"

"Since I woke up." He remembered the dream, and his eyebrows arched. He hurried back to his chair. "I had this dream last night. It was so vivid, John. About some woman looking all over her house for money."

"Money? Sam, are you having financial problems?"

"No! It wasn't about money. It was just a quarter or something. She found it and started celebrating like it was really important. It didn't make any sense. But I'm standing there, part of it, and not part of it . . . wondering what the big deal is with one lost coin."

John sat back in his chair and nodded as if he'd heard all this before. "Sam, did you fall asleep reading the Bible yesterday, by any chance? Had you been reading from Luke 15?"

Sam shook his head. "Luke 15? No. Why?"

"Because I mentioned it in my sermon yesterday. Remember?"

Sam wished he had paid more attention. "No . . . refresh my memory."

John didn't look surprised. "In Luke 15 Jesus tells about a lost coin and a lost sheep and a lost son. It sounds like you were just dreaming about that, maybe processing my sermon."

Sam looked down at his feet. He didn't think it had come out of the Bible—he hadn't read from Luke in a long time. Then he thought about the foreign word that had shaken him so and looked quickly up. "I woke up, and I know I was awake . . . and there was this voice . . . It had all this power and authority, like it was God, himself . . . and he said something in another language."

John's brow furrowed as if he was trying to follow every word. "What did he say?"

"*Ephphatha*, I think. Something like that. You know what that means?"

"No." John thought for a moment. "So that's the voice you heard? That's why you think you're going crazy?"

"No, not just that." Sam got up again and walked across the room, combing his fingers through his sweat-dampened hair. "I was at the diner where I eat breakfast every day, and I heard the waitress—her thoughts or something. I looked up, and she hadn't said anything. And the lady next to me . . . she said gravity was going to let her go, and she was going to fly out in the universe and nobody would notice. I looked at her, and, John, she hadn't said anything. She was just staring down at her coffee. And then the man at the table, and the woman crossing the street, and the elevator guy, and my secretary . . ."

"You heard all of their thoughts?"

"Not their thoughts. I couldn't read their thoughts. Just . . . their feelings, I guess. I don't know." He sat back down. "John, you've got to help me. I don't know what to do."

John took in a deep breath, and looking troubled, he got up and went around his desk. "Sam, I'm gonna refer you to a counselor. You need to talk to a professional."

"Like . . . a shrink?" Sam asked. He remembered telling his wife she needed psychiatric help. He had been kidding, but John was not. The idea didn't thrill him, but he would do anything to get to the bottom of this. A shrink probably saw things like this all the time. Maybe there was some logical explanation. Food poisoning or a bump on the head he'd forgotten about. Maybe he could stop the voices. "That's okay," he said as his mind reeled with possibilities. "That's good. Maybe he can help me."

John flipped through his Rolodex for the name, pulled out a card, and wrote the number. Sam knew he didn't believe him about the voices, but it didn't much matter, as long as he got some help.

"I don't belong in ministry. Nobody listens. I'm not making an impact."

Sam looked up. "Sure, you do."

John stopped writing. "What?"

"You make an impact. You definitely make an impact. You're not thinking of leaving the ministry just because of wackos like me . . . ?"

John's face changed radically, and he sat frozen, staring back at Sam.

Then Sam realized what he had done. "You didn't say anything, did you? You thought it or felt it. I heard it, John. Don't you see?"

John looked as startled as Sam. "I hadn't told anybody that," he said. "I hadn't discussed this even with my wife. It's just been going through my mind . . ."

"I heard it, John! I'm not making this up! Now can you see what I'm going through?"

John was beginning to perspire now. He rubbed his chin for a moment, staring at Sam with stricken eyes. Slowly, he got up, came back around the desk, and sat in the chair opposite Sam. "Sam, can you hear what I'm thinking right now?"

Sam closed his eyes and tried to listen. It was useless. He couldn't hear on demand. He had no power over what was happening to him. "No. I'm not psychic. It's not like that. It's more like I hear . . . needs. Specific ones."

"Needs? Could you hear people's orders in the diner? Before they spoke?"

"No, not those kinds of needs. It's like . . . what you said in church Sunday, about what would happen if we could hear people's spiritual needs."

John sat back in his chair, silent for a moment. "I didn't think you were listening."

"I wasn't," Sam admitted. "It just sort of came back to me this morning. After God spoke that word."

"You really feel it was God who said that to you?"

Again, he struggled to think it through logically but came back to the same conclusion. "Yes, I do think it was God. I mean, think about it. I'm dreaming about Luke 15, I hear a word in some other language, I remember part of your sermon . . . That stuff never happens to me."

"Thanks a lot," John said.

"But I start hearing all these things . . ."

John went to his bookshelf and got down his concordance. "What was the word again?"

"*Ephphtha* or something."

"*Epithet?*"

"No. It wasn't English. I'm sure it wasn't."

"*Ephah?* That's a measurement."

"No. It had another syllable, I think. Let me see." Sam took the book and scanned the *Eph's*, whispering the pronunciation of each word. *"Epher, Ephesus, Ephod . . ."* His eyes widened as he came to the word. *"Ephphatha!* This is it! John, this is the word."

John took the book and found the reference. "It's Mark 7:34." He grabbed up his Bible, scanned the verses, then dropped back into his chair. "Wow."

"What?" Sam took the Bible and found the verse. Slowly, he began to read. "He looked up to heaven and with a deep sigh said to him, *'Ephphatha!'* (which means, 'Be opened!')." Sam frowned up at the pastor. "So what was God trying to say to me?"

"Look at the context," John said. "They had brought Jesus a deaf, mute man. And Jesus spat on his fingers and put them into his ears and said, *'Ephphatha!* Be opened.' And the man began to hear and speak."

"But what has that got to do with me? I'm not even hard of hearing."

John got that look in his eyes that he got when he thought the Holy Spirit was moving in their church services. He was obviously getting excited. "Don't you see, Sam? For some reason, the Lord came to you last night, and he opened your ears. Is it possible, Sam, that you're hearing what the Holy Spirit hears? Out loud?"

Sam sorted back through the things he'd heard and slowly began to nod. "I heard a woman who couldn't provide for her family, another woman who thought she'd never escape her past, somebody who thought she was nobody, insignificant . . ."

"Spiritual needs. Just as God hears them."

Sam thought about it for a moment. "Yes, I guess so. But . . . why me? Why would God choose me to curse?"

"Sam, this isn't a curse! This is a gift!" John said. "What I wouldn't give to have it!"

"But why me? Why not somebody like you who knows how to explain about Jesus? Somebody who's comfortable with sharing their faith?"

"We're all supposed to witness whether we're comfortable or not, Sam. That's what I preached on Sunday. We're all supposed to go out there with the feeling of urgency because there are lost people and no one to find them!"

"*But I can't do that!*" Sam shouted. "I'm just an ordinary guy! I'm not a preacher. I've never been to seminary. What am I supposed to do? Preach on the street corners? Go around proclaiming Jesus from the mountaintops?"

"Yes!" John said, springing to his feet.

Sam let out a disbelieving breath and wilted back into the chair. "John, you've got to help me. I can't do this."

"Sure you can," John said, leaning toward him and taking his shoulder. "Sam, if you're a Christian you can do this. You've been given a mighty gift, and the Lord never gives a gift he doesn't equip you to use."

"But this is insane. Kate'll have me committed."

"Not if she hears her deepest spiritual needs spoken back to her like you just did with me. People will listen to you, Sam! They want nothing more than to find the answers to their deepest needs— they'll *want* you to talk to them! Do you know how special that is?"

Sam felt suddenly overwhelmed. He dropped his face into his hands and began to cry, something he hadn't done since his mother's funeral years ago. This was too much for one man to handle.

John laid his hand on the back of Sam's neck. "Sam, I want to pray for you. This seems like a lot, I know. But God gave it to you. You need to thank him and acknowledge that you can't use it without him. It's *his* power."

Sam could accept that; this wasn't something of his own doing. Only God could have come up with something this amazing. He bowed his head, still crying, and listened as John prayed for him. He wished he could believe that the Lord would just fill him with words and courage and that Sam could tell everyone he saw how to meet those needs, just like Paul or Peter. But he had trouble seeing himself in that role. Since when was Sam Bennett a missionary evangelist? When John whispered, "Amen," Sam looked helplessly up at him.

"Sam, I'll help you," John said. "How about if we each take the day off? We can go somewhere and sit. You can just tell me everything you hear. I'll take it from there. I'll teach you how to let God direct."

Sam felt the first calm of the day washing over him like a warm tide, and he squinted up at John through his tears. "You could do that?"

"Of course I could. I can't wait to see how this works."

He opened his hands. "All right. Where will we go?"

John thought a moment. "The bus station? It's sometimes pretty crowded this time of day. Think of all those lost souls. All those voices."

"No." Sam shook his head adamantly. "I can't handle that. Just a few at a time. Let's go someplace I'm used to. Let's go back to the diner."

"All right," John said. "Let me just leave a note for the staff."

But as they headed back out to John's car, Sam felt a sinking, sick feeling deep in his gut that God had made his first mistake.

4

Since Sam was so distracted, John drove following Sam's directions to the diner. The place was even more crowded than it had been when he'd been here earlier. Sam looked at his watch and realized that it wasn't that late in the day; it was only 9:30 A.M. He'd gotten an awfully early start today. Dozens of people still crammed in to grab breakfast before heading to work.

John followed him in and looked around for a booth. Janie, the waitress, lifted her voice over the noise. "Good thing you came back, Sam, since you ran out of here without paying me this morning."

Sam hadn't thought of it until now. Embarrassed, he made his way to the counter. "I'm sorry, Janie. I wasn't thinking clearly. But you knew I'd be back, didn't you?"

"Sure," Janie said, waving him off. "You've never stiffed me before." She pointed to the booth in the corner. Two orderlies from the hospital were just leaving it. "Why don't you take that one, and I'll get Joe to come out and wipe the table for you. Joe!"

John looked around as if he was a little shell-shocked at the noise and crowd as they took the sticky table. Sam gestured toward Janie as they sat down. "I heard her voice this morning."

"What did it say?" John asked.

"Something about rest. That it could change her whole life. That doesn't sound like a spiritual need to me, does it to you?"

John considered that for a moment. "Jesus said, 'Come to me all ye who are weary and heavy laden, and I will give you rest.'"

Sam rubbed his jaw. "Sure did, didn't he? How about that?"

"So did you tell her that?"

"No, I didn't tell her anything. I didn't know what was happening. It surprised me when I realized she didn't know I'd heard her. And then that lady next to me said that thing about gravity letting her go, and—"

"Is she here now?"

Sam looked around. "No, she's gone."

"So how did you answer her?"

Sam grunted out his annoyance. "I didn't. She got irritated when I tried, so I moved to another table."

"Oh." John was clearly disappointed. "Did you talk to anybody about what you heard?"

"Of course not. They would have called the police or something." He stared across the table at his pastor, wondering what he expected.

"So what are you hearing right now?" John asked.

Sam drew in a deep breath and sat back in his booth, listening.

"I can't do this alone." The voice startled him, and he turned to the table next to theirs and saw a pregnant girl with a toddler.

He turned back to John and tried to cover his mouth. "The woman next to us—she said she can't do this alone."

John's eyes danced like those of a kid at the gates of an amusement park. "Go tell her she doesn't have to."

Sam shifted in his seat. He was sorry he'd ever brought John into this. "I can't do that!"

"Why not?"

"Because. She doesn't know I heard her thoughts. She'll think it's a pickup line."

"No, she won't. If you go up and address her deepest spiritual need, you think she's gonna turn you away?"

"Well, no, but . . . come on, John. I come here every day. I know some of these people. I don't want them to start running from me."

John's expression fell. "He hasn't heard a word I've said." The words didn't come through his lips, and Sam's face grew hot.

He leaned forward, locking eyes with his pastor. "I have too heard what you've said, John. Stop thinking you're a failure because I'm not Billy Graham."

"God isn't asking you to be Billy Graham," John said. "Sam, why do you think God gave you this ability?"

"I don't know. I've been asking myself that all morning. I guess it's punishment for being lukewarm or something."

"It's not a punishment," John whispered. "It's a wonderful gift. What are you afraid of?"

"I don't know. Of messing somebody's head up. Of telling them the wrong thing. Of turning them off to religion altogether because they think I'm some kind of Bible-waving maniac."

John seemed to look right into him. Sam hated that about him. "It's not really any of those things, is it, Sam?"

"You got the gift too?" Sam demanded. "You think you can look into my heart and see what I'm feeling? Well, why don't you just tell me what it is?"

John kept his eyes locked on Sam's. "I think you're embarrassed. Ashamed."

"Ashamed!" He thought of leaving—just storming out in righteous indignation. "I'm not ashamed of my faith!"

"Then how many times have you told anybody else about it?"

"Plenty!" he said. "They can see by my life. People know that I don't do business the same way they do. I treat others kindly. They know I'm active at church. They *know*, okay?"

"But how many times have you shared it out loud? In words? How many people have you led to Christ?"

"None that I know of, but that doesn't mean I'm ashamed. It just means that the situation hasn't come up." He stopped and stared at his preacher across the table. Even without his gift, Sam knew what John was thinking. He was making excuses. Sam rubbed his face. "Look, John, there's nothing I'd like better than to be able to say I've led a bunch of people to Christ. Every Christian would like to think that. But I'm not like you. That's not my gift. I'm not bold that way. I mean, what if I get over there and start telling that woman about Jesus, and she asks me some theological question that I can't answer, because frankly—and I'll just be honest here—I haven't studied the Bible all that much."

"Do you know Jesus?" John asked.

Sam looked at him, astonished. "Yes, John! Can you really ask me that? You baptized me. I may not be the greatest Christian who ever lived, but I do have a relationship with Christ."

"Then tell her about that," John said. "That's all she needs to know right now. That's all *you* need to know right now."

Sam couldn't believe the pastor was putting him on the spot this way. Did John think it was that simple? "I don't even know how to start the conversation. I mean, what do I do? Go plop down at her table and tell her that she doesn't have to do this alone? What if she doesn't even realize that was what she was thinking? What if—"

John's eyes were laughing. "You know, Sam, Satan doesn't have to do anything to foil your attempts to get the word out. You're doing his job for him."

Sam leaned back hard in his booth. "Oh, that's low. That's really low, John."

"Why do you think God is letting you hear these voices?"

He clenched his hands into fists. "To drive me crazy."

"No," John said. "He obviously wants you to respond to them. You wouldn't just be hearing these things if you weren't supposed to respond in some way."

"So you're saying that every time I hear these voices I'm supposed to launch into some kind of amateur sermon?"

"Maybe that's the plan."

"I probably heard six voices at one time in the grocery store. Was I supposed to climb up on an egg crate and start preaching to them?"

"You tell me."

"Come on, John!"

John looked over at the woman, and Sam followed his gaze. She was helping the child eat some hash browns while her other hand rubbed the top of her belly. "I'm scared," Sam heard her say, though she hadn't really said it. "I don't want to do this."

He wondered if she was headed to the hospital for an appointment. If there was a husband in her life. If she really was alone or just *felt* alone. Suddenly, he forgot where he and John were in their argument.

John had obviously forgotten too. The pastor slid out of the booth.

Sam caught his arm. "Where are you going?"

"Just right here to talk to this lady," he whispered.

Sam let go and watched John approach her. "Ma'am, I'm John Ingalls, Pastor of Church of the Savior over on Post Road," he said gently, "and I was just noticing this precious little girl."

The young woman smiled. "Thank you."

"Do you mind if I sit down for just a second? I'd like to talk to you if you have a minute."

She shrugged. "Sure, go ahead."

That was it, Sam thought. That was the place where he would have struck out. She would have taken one look at him and yelled for help. He'd often had that effect on women.

But John had that kind, non-threatening face. It was clear from a mile away that the man was a preacher.

Janie brought Sam coffee, and he began meticulously mixing the sugar and cream into it as he listened to the conversation at the next table.

"I noticed the way you kept rubbing your stomach," John said. "I just wondered if you're all right."

She breathed a laugh. "Well, frankly, I may not be."

"What do you mean?"

"I'm kind of in labor."

Sam's head came up.

"Why aren't you in the hospital?" John asked.

"I've been there already," she said. "They told me I'm just in the early stages. That I should come back when the contractions are closer together. They said to walk around a little, relax . . ."

"Well, have you notified your husband?"

She shook her head. "I don't have a husband."

"Well, the baby's father, then. Isn't there—?"

Tears sprang to her eyes, and she put her hand over her mouth. The little girl looked up at her, touched her, as if the tears were familiar, yet still dreadful.

John leaned forward on the table and met her eyes. "You must be feeling pretty alone right now."

Sam's eyes shot across to John. He was using what Sam had told him about her need. She nodded fiercely. "That's exactly how I'm feeling."

"Do you have someone to keep this sweet little girl while you're in the hospital?"

She wiped her eyes. "No. Social Services is going to take her until I get out. I don't see why she can't just stay there with me. She's real good . . ." Her voice trailed off as she put her arm around the tiny child's shoulders.

John was shaking his head. "Look, my wife and I would love to baby-sit for you while you're in the hospital. We love kids, and our baby just went off to college this year. She could stay with us for as long as you want her to."

The prospect seemed to trouble her more. She took the child's hand and laced their fingers together. "Thank you, but I don't know . . ."

"Of course you wouldn't trust me just like that," John said. "Call my church and ask about me. I could get my wife to come here so you could meet her. If you don't feel good about us after all that, then we'll just go our separate ways and leave you alone."

She stared across the table. "Why would you do that? Baby-sit for someone you've never met?"

"Because something told me that you were alone and you

needed it. And to be perfectly honest, I needed an opening so I could explain to you that you're not really alone, that there's someone who loved you enough to die for you. And because he loves you so much, he sat me down at the table next to you, so I could come and tell you."

As if he was the one to whom John referred, she looked over at Sam, still alone at the next table. "Someone loved me?" she asked, almost disgusted. "Who?"

"Jesus Christ," he said.

Her face changed, and he saw the cynicism that lined her young face. "Oh, come on. Give me a break."

"No, listen to me," John said, brooking no debate. "You are not alone. You may feel like you are, but there are people out there who can love you and care for you, and the only reason they can is that Jesus does."

She rubbed her stomach. "If only I could believe that."

"You can believe it," he said. "It's true."

The woman's face began to redden, and it twisted as she began to weep. The little girl set down her spoon and stared up at her mother. John touched the woman's shoulder. "Ma'am, this doesn't have to go on, this feeling of solitude. When you bring that baby into the world today, you could bring it into a Christian home."

She looked down at her stomach, then over at the child. "I've never taken her to church," she said. "I've never taught her anything about the Bible. There's so much I would have to learn."

"You don't have to learn anything before you come to Christ," John said. "All you have to do is pray and tell Jesus that you want him to take over your life. Do you want to do that?"

Still weeping, she nodded her head. "It couldn't be any worse than it's been." She breathed in a sob. "Yes, I'd like to do that."

John met Sam's eyes, quietly saying, *See? You could do this.* But Sam knew better—John was a natural. "Let's pray," John said.

She looked awkwardly around her. "I don't know if I can do this right out in public . . ."

"He died right out in public," John whispered. "Don't let embarrassment keep you from that kind of love."

John closed his eyes, and the woman followed. Sam listened as John began to lead her in prayer, and he felt the thrill of witnessing a new convert being ushered into the kingdom of God. He couldn't believe it had been so easy. He'd heard stories of doors being slammed in people's faces, persecutions, even. He'd read about that in the Bible.

Then the thought came to him. *I've made it easy for you, Sam.*

He drew in a deep breath as they came out of the prayer, and the tension on the woman's face began to drain away as she laughed through her tears. She was not much more than a teenager, he realized. Practically a kid. About his daughter's age. His heart jolted at the thought of Jennifer, a college freshman, in labor with no one beside her. How could that have happened to this young woman?

John kept talking to her, and after a moment, he got up and went to the pay phone. Sam knew he was calling his wife to come and get the little girl. He wondered how often John put Christ's love into such concrete action. Maybe that was what they were all supposed to do, he thought. Maybe Christians, like doctors, were supposed to heal fatal spiritual ills, terminal diseases of the soul.

When John came back, he put Sam on the spot. "Sam, come

here for a minute. I want you to meet the newest member of our family."

Sam got awkwardly up and reached for her hand.

"You're brothers?" the woman asked.

"No," Sam said quickly.

"Brothers in Christ," John said. "And now you're our sister."

Her eyes filled again as she laughed softly. "Oh. Right."

Sam sat down at the table. He didn't know what to say.

The child stood up, revealing her wet pants. "Uh-oh," she said. "We haven't quite got this potty training down." She got to her feet, her hand on her stomach. "Would you all excuse me for a minute, please? I'm leaving my bag here."

Sam looked under the table and saw her duffel bag for the hospital. She carried a diaper bag and purse on her shoulder.

"If you'd just keep an eye on it, I'll be right back."

"Sure," John said. "Are you sure you'll be all right?"

"Oh, yeah. I've probably got hours yet. I'll just yell out if anything happens."

They disappeared into the rest room, and John grinned back at Sam. "So what do you think about that?"

"I think that was amazing," Sam said. "The most amazing thing I've ever seen."

"You could do it too. It's very simple. You know their needs. Address them."

But Sam was still skeptical. It was one thing to know their needs. It was another to meet them.

"I'm so dirty." The voice behind him was as loud as if it had been whispered right in his ear, and he turned around and saw the man sitting there, in a clean, pressed suit, reading the newspaper as if nothing was wrong. "I can't stand my life anymore. I'm filthy, tainted."

Sam turned back to John. "The man behind me," he said. "He said he feels dirty, tainted, filthy."

John's serious eyes locked into his. "Go tell him, Sam. Tell him how he can get clean."

Sam closed his eyes. He didn't want to be here. He didn't want this responsibility on him, this accountability. He was getting a headache. He needed to lie down.

"Go on," the pastor urged.

Sam rubbed his temples. "You better do it," he said. "You've had more experience with this sort of thing."

"Sam, just talk to him."

"What do I say?" he whispered harshly. "How do I lead in? 'Excuse me, but I couldn't help overhearing your soul crying out?'"

"No," John said. "Just tell him what happened to you."

Sam sighed as the woman and her child made their way back to the table. John obviously needed to keep talking to her about her newfound faith and the baby on the way. Sam realized he was stuck. If he didn't do it, his pastor would think he was a coward. Slowly, he got up and turned to the chair behind him. "Excuse me," he said.

The man looked up from the newspaper. "Yeah?"

"I'm sorry to bother you," Sam said. "I'm just . . . well, you see, I kind of have this gift, and I can sort of . . . hear things . . ."

The man's eyes narrowed. He wasn't following what Sam was saying. Sam put his hand on the chair and started to pull it out. "May I?"

The man leaned suspiciously back in his chair. "Sure, go ahead."

"Well, you see, I couldn't help overhearing . . ."

The man was quiet, waiting.

". . . something you may not realize you said." Sam stopped and realized he was taking the wrong route. He didn't need to be quite that direct.

"I'm sorry; I don't understand."

"Of course you don't. Uh . . . look, man." He leaned his elbows on the table and got closer, keeping his voice confidentially low. "This isn't going to make any sense to you, but I felt like I should come over here and tell you something about myself."

The man looked as if he was bracing himself for a sales pitch.

"A few years ago . . . I did some things . . . saw some things . . . put some things into my head that . . . well, they just made me feel really dirty."

The man's face changed. Sam knew he had his attention.

"I don't want to go into the details," Sam said. "But let me just say that I really felt that I couldn't stand my life anymore. I got to the point where I thought that if there was a God, he must be awfully disgusted with me."

The man sat stone still . . . listening.

"And then one night I was sitting at home with my wife, who's this strong Christian woman, and she'd been dragging me to church by the hand for years and years . . . and I just about lost it. I started to cry, and I couldn't stop crying, and I began to confess to her everything I was doing. My wife . . . she got up and got her Bible and opened it to this one section I'd never seen before." He shrugged. "Of course I hadn't seen it. I never listened in church, never paid any attention, never read it. But it said that while we were yet sinners, Christ died for us."

The man looked down at the table. His hands were trembling. Sam was getting to him, he thought. It was working.

"And it really got to me, you see, because there I was telling my wife my darkest secrets, not thinking even she could forgive me, and there she was telling me that somebody died for me, to take my punishment for all the filth, even when I was his enemy."

The man's nostrils flared. He closed his hands into fists over his newspaper and brought his eyes up to Sam's. "Are you finished?"

Sam's heart sank. He'd thought he had him, but now it was clear he'd gone too far. "Well . . . yes. I just wanted to tell you because—"

"Then would you kindly let me eat in peace?" the man bit out.

Sam didn't know what to say. Confused, he scooted his chair back. "Yeah, sure. Okay. But . . . if you ever want to talk or anything . . ."

"To you?" the man asked with disdain. He almost laughed. "Thanks, pal. But if I ever needed to talk, it wouldn't be to some born-again sleazeball who peddles his religion like cheap watches. I have a life." With that, he folded his newspaper and got up.

Sam dug into his pocket for his business card. "Look, just take this, in case you ever—"

"Didn't you hear me, pal? I don't need what you're selling."

"Yes, you do."

The man laughed then. Shaking his head, he tossed down some money for his meal, and bolted out the door.

Sam felt as if the wind had been knocked out of him. He stayed at the table, running the conversation back through his mind, trying to figure out where he had gone wrong.

Later, when John's wife had come and taken the little girl home and her mother had gone for a walk to speed up her contractions, Sam and John left the diner. "I guess I failed pretty miserably in there, didn't I?" Sam asked.

John gave him an amused look across the hood of the car. "You've got to be kidding. You were great."

"Great? That guy practically ran out. It couldn't have gone worse."

"But that's not your fault. The Lord revealed the man's need to you, and you were obedient and responded. If he rejected it, he's accountable to God, not you."

"How do you know that?"

Before Sam knew what was happening, John had whipped a small Bible out of his shirt pocket and was turning to Ezekiel. "Says so right here. Chapter 3 of Ezekiel." He slid the Bible across the seat. "Read for yourself. Verses 18 and 19."

Sam took the Bible and began to mumble the words. "When I say to a wicked man, 'You will surely die,' and you do not warn him or speak out to dissuade him from his evil ways in order to save his life, that wicked man will die for his sin, and I will hold you accountable for his blood."

Sam stopped on the last word, suddenly remembering the woman with the red braid this morning, walking through traffic with no regard for her life. He hadn't told her what he knew. If she'd been hit by that skidding car and died without knowing Christ, he would have been accountable.

He felt the blood drain from his face.

"Read on," John said. "Just the next verse."

"But if you do warn the wicked man and he does not turn from his wickedness or from his evil ways . . ."

"Like the guy who just rejected you," John interjected.

". . . he will die for his sin; but you will have saved yourself."

"You won't be accountable," John said, "because you warned him."

"Well, that's fine for me," Sam said. "But what about him? Why wouldn't he listen if I addressed his real spiritual need?"

"Some won't ever listen," John said. "There will always be those who reject the truth. That can't stop us."

Sam closed his eyes and leaned his head against the window. "I still feel like a failure. If I'd gone about it another way . . . approached him differently. . . What good is this gift?"

"It did the woman good," John said. "I wouldn't have known what she needed if you hadn't told me."

"Still . . . you were right about me, John. I'm pitiful. I've been a Christian for ten years, and not once in those ten years have I ever led anybody to Christ. Until about an hour ago, I never even wanted to."

"Well, don't look now, but I think things are about to change. With this gift, God is leading you straight to the front lines."

Sam was silent for several moments. "I don't know if I'm ready for this, John."

"Sam, God doesn't wait for you to be ready. Sometimes he just throws you in. It's not a real hard thing, talking about Jesus. You don't have to take a class; you don't have to read a book; you don't have to memorize an outline. All you really have to do is tell them what he did for you. That's the best testimony there is."

Sam nodded his head slowly and wished that he had the confidence and passion that John had. Instead, he had a sick feeling that he was going to let the Lord down. The angels in heaven were probably bracing themselves in dread at all the damage he was about to do.

5

After much persuading, John convinced Sam to join him on his hospital visits. As they walked across the street, Sam began to feel uneasy again. "You know, I'm not very good with sick people. I hope you plan to do all the talking. I think I almost gave that guy at the diner a heart attack. His face was beet red when I got through with him."

John didn't seem worried. In fact, Sam could almost see the wheels turning in his head. "One of my greatest frustrations as a pastor is when members of my flock are about to die and I can't look into their spirit and tell for sure if they know the Lord. That's why I want you to come. I think it would help me a lot if you could just tell me what you hear when you sit in their room, so I'll know which way to lead the conversation and how to address their needs."

"But I can't just repeat back to you what I hear," Sam said. "They'd get wise."

"Wise to what?" John asked. "Wise to the fact that someone knew their spiritual needs? That last guy is proof that they're not even thinking these things consciously. You could probably repeat them right back to them verbatim, and they may not even recognize them."

"You recognized them when I repeated your needs."

"But I'm already a Christian. I've prayed about what you heard. I've looked my problems in the face."

Sam couldn't help remembering the needs he'd heard in John. "You aren't really thinking about leaving the ministry, are you?"

Several moments passed before John answered. "Yeah, actually, I am."

"Why? I thought you loved preaching."

"I love serving the Lord. But if I'm not making an impact, then I need to get out of it. It's a frustrating profession sometimes, Sam. You stand up in that pulpit, pouring out your heart and soul, and half the congregation just stares back at you with glassy eyes, trying to stifle their yawns. Five minutes after the sermon they can't remember what your main point was. Churches are supposed to grow. Christians are supposed to bear fruit. If neither of those things is happening in my church, then I'm failing."

Sam gaped at him. "I don't get it. You're not failing—how do you figure that? Our church is vibrant. It's great."

John breathed a cynical laugh. "Yeah, we did win the citywide basketball championship this year, and our softball team is shaping up to be a winner. But that's not what I'm going for. It's all those pesky lost souls that are troubling me. And all those yawning Christians who don't care about them."

"Oh, come on," Sam said. "I care. But this stuff is hard. I mean, you just said that lots of people don't even know their deepest spiritual needs. If they don't, what's the point? I mean, what can you really do? Even this so-called gift I have, how does it help if they don't recognize their needs when I mention them?"

"The point is that their soul would recognize them. Something inside them would stir, whether they admit it or not. These people we're going to visit in the hospital . . . some of them are scared. They need to know what Jesus can do to help them."

"But don't they have enough problems, being sick and all?"

John shot him a look. "Some of them are going to die. This may be their last chance. That's part of the reason why I insist on visiting members of my church. I don't want anybody to die without understanding completely."

Sam got quiet, thoughtful, as they walked the rest of the way to the hospital. His wife worked here as a nurse, and as they went in, he was assaulted with the mingling smells of sterility and disease. He knew other people couldn't smell it, but it always seemed to jump out at him. That was why he avoided hospitals like the plague. His mother had died in a room on the fourth floor, and he hadn't been back since. Whenever he picked up Kate, she met him in the parking lot.

He wondered what his wife would say about his being here now, or about this bizarre gift he'd been cursed with. This morning, when they'd had coffee together, he hadn't known about it. Why hadn't he heard her needs? His mind ran back through their conversation.

I just want to be useful.

The words scampered through his mind. He'd heard her say that, but now that he thought about it, he hadn't been looking at her. Had she really said it, or had she felt it?

John glanced over at him as they reached the elevator. "You okay?"

"Yeah," Sam said. "I'm fine. I was just wondering if I should tell Kate."

"Why keep it secret from her?"

"I don't know. She might feel violated, knowing I can hear right into her."

John grinned. "Are you kidding? That's every woman's dream. To know that her life partner can hear her deepest needs. The problem will be convincing her, but if you do what you did with me this morning, she'll believe you."

The elevator doors opened, and John stepped on. Sam was beginning to get that sick feeling again. "Who are we visiting?"

"Annabelle York."

"Do I know her?"

"She's old. She's been homebound for a while, but until a few months ago she sat in the front row and said 'Amen' to everything I said."

"Oh, yeah. The little white-haired lady. She has been out for a while, hasn't she?" He was ashamed that he hadn't thought of her until now.

"She's got cancer of the liver. They've done everything they can do."

"Well, you're not worried about her spiritual condition, are you? I mean, she's obviously a Christian."

"Maybe, but you can't ever tell. You know what the Bible says. Not everyone who calls 'Lord, Lord,' will enter the kingdom of heaven."

The doors opened, but Sam made no move to get off. "Why would she come to church every Sunday, sit in the front row, shout out 'Amen,' if she wasn't really a Christian?"

"I'm not saying that's the case," John said, catching the elevator door before it could shut. "If I were the judge, I'd say this woman's got it lock, stock, and barrel. But the problem is, a lot of times they fool you. A lot of times they fool themselves. I just don't like taking chances when someone's about to leave the world. I want you to tell me what you hear."

They got off the elevator, and Sam began to feel the dread he'd always felt when he'd approached his mother's room. He looked for an exit door as they walked. "John, how am I gonna do this? I can't just tell you what I hear in front of her."

"Find some way to pose it. I don't care how you do it. Just do it. I need to know."

Once again, Sam resented this gift that he hadn't asked for and didn't want. He slowed as they approached the door to her room. John knocked, and when he didn't hear an answer, pushed the door open, and stuck his head in. "Miss Annabelle, how are you doing, sweetheart?"

Sam grudgingly followed him in. This was rude, he thought, shoving his way into somebody's hospital room when they weren't feeling well. But it was too late to stop the pastor. John was at the bed, leaning over it. The old woman smiled and reached up to take his hand. He squeezed it and asked her softly how she was doing. The woman could barely speak.

"You remember Sam from church, don't you, Miss Annabelle? He's making the rounds with me today."

She smiled weakly and nodded her head, as if she knew him well, but Sam wasn't sure he'd ever been close enough to look her in the eye. "How are you, ma'am?"

"Fine," she mouthed, as if too weak to project. Then he heard a strong voice that wasn't coming from her lips. "It's too late. Way too late. So many years wasted."

Sam took a step back and tried to signal John with his eyes that he'd heard something. Then he realized that if he leaned over and whispered to John, she probably didn't even have the strength to notice.

John's eyes riveted into Sam's, and he nodded for him to pass it on.

"She thinks it's too late," Sam said quietly, and he saw her looking at him, straining to hear. "She thinks she's wasted years."

John frowned as if he didn't know what to make of that. "But does she know the Lord?" John whispered.

As if in answer, the voice came again. "All the people I could have taken to heaven with me. But I was more concerned about doing that busy church work and keeping a clean house."

Yes, Sam thought. She knew Christ. At once, a boldness overtook him and he wanted to talk to her, to help her. He didn't want to play games by whispering to John. He stepped around the bed and got closer to her. "Miss Annabelle," he said. "The Lord has revealed something about you to me. Do you mind if I tell you what it is?"

She shook her head.

"The Lord told me that you're concerned because you didn't lead more people to Christ. That you feel you were more preoccupied with church work and housework than with soul winning."

Her eyes brimmed with tears, and her mouth came open as she tried to speak. She looked from Sam to the preacher and squeezed his hand. "Think . . . how many people . . . I could have helped."

John bent down over her, still holding her gnarled hand. "Miss Annabelle, let me pray for you."

Sam bowed his head as John began to pray for the old woman who was suffering her last hours of life on earth and worrying about coming face to face with the One who knew her original potential.

Later, when they were back out in the hall, John smiled softly. "Miss Annabelle will be in heaven soon."

"Yes, she will," Sam said. "She's definitely a Christian. But she seemed so sad about what she hadn't done."

"I think a lot of us are going to feel that way when we get to the end," John said. "I see that a lot."

They went on to the next room that John had on his list. "Who are we gonna see now?" Sam asked.

"Sid Beautral. You know, Hattie Beautral's husband?"

Sam frowned. "I thought she was a widow."

"No, she just comes alone. He's not big on church. He had gall-bladder surgery."

"So he's not dying?"

"No, just recovering."

"Thank goodness," Sam said. They paused at the door and John knocked. A woman called, "Come in."

John pushed the door open. "Hello, Miss Hattie. How are you, Sid?"

John hugged the woman easily, then shook the hand of the man in bed. It seemed second nature to John to embrace the weak, while Sam found creative ways to avoid them.

"What brings you here, Preacher?" the man asked gruffly. "You know I ain't dying."

"Of course you're not," John said. "I don't just visit dying people. I visit anybody in my flock who's in the hospital."

"You count me in your flock?" he asked skeptically.

"Yes, believe it or not, I do. Now, how are you doing?"

Sid shrugged. "Guess I'm okay."

Then Sam heard his voice again, but Sid's lips didn't move. "I'm powerless. Can't defend myself. All my life is in somebody else's control."

Sam nudged John. John nodded, encouraging him to speak. Sam cleared his throat and tapped his hand nervously on the bedrail. "Uh . . . Mr. Beautral, you're probably feeling pretty powerless lying here, like you're not in control . . . like you can't defend yourself."

"Defend myself from what?" the man asked, his eyes narrowing.

Sam was at a loss. "From anything. I don't know. What threatens you?"

The man looked as if he thought Sam was crazy. "Nothing threatens me. I mean, nothing I can think of."

Fortunately, John took it from there, and Sam let out a heavy breath and stepped back. "Sid, you know you don't have to feel powerless," John said. "There is someone in control, and it's someone who loves you and knows the number of hairs on your head."

Miss Hattie smiled, and the man looked up at him, his face changing as his eyes locked into John's. Sam prayed that John would lead this man to Christ before they left here today.

When they got back into the car to leave the hospital, John's eyes were dancing. "I think this has got to be one of the best days of my Christian life."

Sam wished he felt so exuberant, but every muscle in his body was as rigid as stone. He knew the tension would take hours to subside. "I think it's probably one of the worst days of my Christian life," he admitted.

"Why?" John asked. "Don't you feel good knowing that you'll never get to the point where Miss Annabelle is, getting to the end of your life and feeling regret because you never led anyone to Christ? Look at how many people we've influenced just this morning."

"*You've* influenced," Sam said. "I haven't really done anything except repeat back what I've heard."

"You've done more than you know. You've listened, Sam. Not everybody listens."

"Not everybody has to hear what I hear," Sam muttered. "What am I gonna do with this now? How am I gonna get used to this?"

"Maybe you won't ever. Maybe you'll be known as the guy who can nail people's souls. There are worse things people could say about you."

"I don't want that reputation. Or that gift, or whatever you call it. I'm not ready for this."

"Of course you are. If I were to leave you right now at the bus station and you went in there and all those people were standing around, you'd know just what to do."

"No, I wouldn't," he said. "It would freak me out. This morning in the grocery store when I was hearing all those voices at the same time all around me, I thought I was losing my mind."

"Well, if it was possible for you to transfer the gift to me, I'd take it before you could say *Ephphatha*."

Sam was exhausted by the time John agreed to return to the church. As John went in, Sam got into his car and sat there a moment, thinking. He knew he couldn't handle going to the office, so he called Sally on his cell phone and told her he would be out the rest of the day.

"I bought the lottery ticket, Sam," she said. "Maybe you ought to start looking for another secretary."

He closed his eyes and dropped his head to the steering wheel. "How about I wait until you've gotten the check?"

"All right," she said. "But I can't promise two weeks' notice."

He clicked off the cell phone and thought of the need he'd heard in her that morning. *"Eleven, six, fifty-seven . . . It has to win. It has to!"*

What if it did? He had heard it out loud, without her uttering the words. It didn't fit the category of "spiritual need" like all the other things he'd heard today. Maybe she was onto something.

He withdrew a pad of paper from his glove compartment and jotted down the numbers—11, 6, 57. He wondered if it was too late to buy a ticket.

He started the car and headed to the closest convenience store that sold lottery tickets, pulled into the parking lot, and idled there for a moment. Then he remembered the rest of what her soul had said.

"If I win, he'll see what I'm worth."

Was that why he'd heard the numbers? Because they were part of her spiritual need?

Could winning the lottery really be someone's spiritual need? Or was it just God's way of giving him an insider's tip?

Eleven, six, fifty-seven.

What was the jackpot this week? How would Sally feel about having to split it with him? Would she feel betrayed, or amazed? And what would his wife think? Would she accept the money when she was so opposed to the lottery, or would she understand that this new gift gave him vital information that he might as well use? Besides, being wealthy could give him more time to help others.

Suddenly, his runaway thoughts screeched to a halt. What he'd heard had been vital information, all right, but he knew deep down that it was not so he could win the lottery. It was so he could win souls to Christ.

He must be crazy. Either that, or Satan was trying to get in on the act. He closed his eyes and asked God for forgiveness.

Maybe hunger and fatigue, when added to his stress, had been the lethal combination that had driven him to such foolishness. He didn't need a lottery ticket anymore than Sally did. He needed food. Two visits to the diner, and he still hadn't eaten. He and John had been too busy going from one place to another, like Paul and Silas, full of the good news and not enough time to tell everyone about it.

We cannot help speaking about what we have seen and heard. It was a quote he had seen when his Sunday school class studied Acts, and it had jumped out at him then. He'd been convicted that there was something wrong with Christians who *could* stop speaking about what they had seen and heard.

But he was one of them. He'd felt bad about that for half a day, and then he'd gotten over it.

Was this how the Lord was disciplining him? God had struck Paul blind to bring him around. Maybe Sam didn't have so much to complain about.

He started the car and decided to head back to the diner for the third time that day. Janie, the waitress, was still behind the counter, accommodating all her customers with the economy of motion of a seasoned waitress. Sam quietly took a table in the corner, away from anyone he could hear, and watched Janie as she waited on the last of the customers. He remembered what she'd said this morning about needing rest—or what her *soul* had said—and realized that something wasn't right in her life. She had a need.

When she'd finally finished with all those customers, she came back to his table. "Sam, I'm starting to think you have a crush on me. Coming in here three times in one day? Aren't you married?"

Sam chuckled. "Yep, I am. It's been a weird day, Janie."

"Aren't you working today?"

"I guess I'm taking the day off. I'm not feeling my best."

"I'm sorry. You're not contagious, are you? I can't afford to get sick."

He grinned. "If only I were."

She frowned. "Huh?"

"Never mind."

She pulled out her menu pad. "Well, what'll it be this time?"

"A hamburger," he said. "With everything. And how about taking a break and keeping me company while I eat it?"

Her mouth dropped open. "What would your wife say?"

"She would agree that you look like you need a rest. For a few minutes, at least."

Her smile faded, and she looked down at him. He wondered if she realized that was what she needed. "Man, I sure could use a rest. Okay, Sam, I'll be right back."

She came back in moments with his meal and a glass of her own iced tea and sat down across from him, gratefully sighing a breath of relief. "It has been some day in here."

"Tell me about it," he said.

She laughed and looked into her iced tea.

"No, I'm serious. I really want you to tell me about it."

She looked up at him, and in that moment he heard the voice again. "I can't go on like this. Everything's going to fall apart."

"It's just been busy," she said aloud. "My feet are killing me."

His brow knit together in concern. "You don't feel like you can go on, do you?" he asked. "Like everything's just going to fall apart."

She frowned and leaned back in her seat. "How did you know that?"

"Have you ever heard the Bible verse . . . I don't even know for sure where it's found. But it's when Jesus said, 'Come to me all ye who are weary . . . something-or-other . . . and I will give you rest.'"

As he watched her slow reaction, he mentally kicked himself for being so inept with Scripture. Had he really said "something-or-other"? He might as well give it up right now, he thought. He didn't have a chance of leading her to Christ.

"Say that again?" she asked.

He wanted to groan. He couldn't make himself ad-lib again, so he decided to paraphrase. "Jesus said to come to him, and he will give you rest."

"I've heard about that kind of rest," Janie said. "Six feet under."

"No," Sam chuckled. "He means rest now, here. And help with your burdens."

She laughed, but her heart didn't seem to be in it. "No offense, Sam, but I'm handling my burdens just fine."

"Then why are you so soul weary?"

"Soul weary?" Janie asked. "Who says I'm soul weary?"

"I just have this feeling. Jesus said that he came to give us abundant life—he meant you too, Janie."

"What does that mean? Abundant life?"

"Life so full that it just runs over."

"My life is running over, all right. I have spills all over the place."

"But it could be running over with living water." The words surprised even him.

Now she was quiet as she mulled that over. The toughness in her face seemed to melt away, and she seemed to have trouble speaking. "Living water, huh? Abundant life? Rest?" He wasn't sure, but he thought she was blinking back tears. "Tell you the truth, those sound pretty good."

His heart jolted. Had the Scripture, even poorly quoted, really gotten to her? Was it possible that she was receptive to Jesus despite his sorry attempt to help her? Maybe he really could do this!

"See . . . I sometimes lie awake at night," she was saying, "and have to get up so early, and I'm so tired—"

"Why do you lie awake nights?" he cut in.

Her eyes grew distant. "I just lie there, thinking."

"About what?"

"About everything falling apart." Her eyes widened as she realized he had said that a moment earlier. "I just keep thinking that nothing's ever going to get better, that things will just keep breaking down until they get worse and worse and worse."

"What things?" he asked.

She covered her eyes and shook her head. "I can't believe I'm talking to you like this." She drew in a deep breath. "My life," she said. She looked down at the wood grain on the table, then brought her moist eyes back to his. "I'm supposed to be cheering you up. That's what you tip me for."

"You do cheer me up," he said. "But if it's all an act, then what's in it for you?"

Her grin faded to aggravation. "No offense, Sam, but what do you care? You come in here every single day, and you've never said more than, 'Hi, how are you?' and I ask if you want the usual, and you say, 'Yes,' and then you eat, and pay me, and go."

"Well, maybe that was the old me."

She laughed again. "The old you? You mean there's a 'new, improved you'?"

"Let's just say there's a new me. I don't know if it's improved or not. Time will tell." If she only knew, he thought.

"And what do you blame this newness on?" she asked sarcastically.

He knew she was teasing him, but it didn't matter. "Jesus Christ," he said.

She rolled her eyes and nodded as if she'd heard it all before. "No, really."

He smiled. "Yes, really. I'm serious. I've been a Christian for a few years now. But last night something happened. I had a dream."

"A dream?" she repeated. "What happened in your dream?"

He leaned forward on the table. She didn't look away. "The Lord spoke to me. He started making me care about the condition of people's souls. And today I've found out that there are frightened souls, empty souls, guilty souls, tired souls . . ."

Her eyes filled up with tears, and she looked away. He had never seen her cry before. He didn't know if he was going to cry now too, but something about those incipient tears grabbed his heart. He didn't know what to say next. He wished his wife was here, so she could try this from a woman's perspective. He wished he had his Bible or a tract that he could toss at her and run.

He was shaking, fearful that he'd upset her more, but he made himself speak. "Janie, don't you want that rest?"

"If I understood how it could happen, I'd take it in a minute," she said. "But just because the Bible said it doesn't mean it's true."

"Because the Bible said it is the *best* reason to believe it's true."

"You believe that?" she asked.

He nodded.

"So what do I have to do? Start going to church? Change how I dress? Do my hair different? Quit going out with men?"

He shrugged. "Hey, do I look like I have a list of rules on me?"

"Isn't that what Christianity is about? Rules?"

"No way. It is not a list of dos and don'ts. It's about God choosing you because he loves you."

"*Choosing* me?" she asked. "Heaven forbid that God should choose me for anything."

He took a bite of his hamburger and chewed. It bought him a couple of minutes. Finally, he spoke again. "Janie, let me tell you how much God loves you."

"Yeah, you tell me," she said, almost mocking.

"Enough to send his only Son to die for you."

She smirked. "See, that's what I don't get. I've never asked anybody to die for me. And when you Christians say that stuff about God sending his only son to die for me, my first question is why? What's the point in that?"

"He died for your sins, and for mine. Because of those sins, we're all destined for hell, but Jesus came to seek and to save that which was lost, and all we have to do is believe in him, and we can change our direction."

"I know an awful lot of people who believe in Jesus," she said. "They're some of the people I drink with at night. Some of the men who try to come home with me. Some of the ones who gamble on the boats. They have 'Honk if you love Jesus' bumper stickers and those little fish symbols on their cars. But they're not a whole lot different from me."

"You got that right."

She squinted at him, obviously surprised. "What?"

"They *should* be different, but you're right about their being a bunch of sinners. Christians are sinners saved by grace."

"And what is that supposed to mean? See, I hear this saved-by-grace stuff on the radio every Sunday, but for the life of me, I can't figure out what it means."

"It means that while we were sinners, Christ died for us, because God promised he would punish sin. We didn't deserve to have Christ pay that penalty for us, and we still don't deserve it. But it doesn't make it any less true. And just because some Christians are hypocrites and just because some of us let God down, it doesn't change any of it. The bottom line is that Christ is true. And he sent me here three times today to talk to you."

She shot him a disbelieving look. "He didn't send you here to talk to me. He sent you for breakfast and lunch."

"Sorry, Janie, but the food's not that good. He sent me because your soul is tired and because there's rest waiting for you."

Her eyes were growing misty again. "Yeah? And how do I get it?"

"By just believing." He shifted in his seat. "Not just recognizing your need, but *clinging* to God to meet your need. Holding on to him for dear life. Embracing him."

"So you're saying that if you believe with all your heart, it makes you different."

"That's exactly what I'm saying. Not a bunch of rules. Just clinging." He smiled and leaned across the table. "The thing is that when you believe, when you really believe, the Holy Spirit will start making changes in you, not because of a list of rules, but because he loves you and wants the very best for you."

"Humph," she said. "I don't know about that." She scratched a spot off of the table with her fingernail. "You know, you ought to be careful. You start talking to somebody like me about God, and the next thing you know, I might actually show up at your church."

"Why would that be a bad thing?"

She shrugged and combed her fingers through the black roots of her bleached hair. "I'm not exactly the kind of person who was raised in Sunday school."

"Neither am I," he said. "Even as a believer, sometimes I'm not the type. But God's working on me. He hasn't given up on me yet, and he hasn't given up on you, either."

She seemed to be considering his words. "So it's not a crush or your stomach that brought you here three times today?"

"Nope. I came because God loves you."

"See, those two things—God and love—don't go together. My picture of God is of a ruler with a big stick, striking down everybody who makes him mad. And I seem to have a knack for that."

"Your picture is wrong. Jesus told a story about a son who took his inheritance and squandered it away on parties and sinful living until he lost everything and had to take a job feeding pigs."

Janie looked around her. "Yep, I can relate to that."

"He realized how much better off he was with his father, so he went back home to ask his father to hire him. He figured his father would never welcome him back into the family, but he hoped he would at least give him a job. But his father saw him coming from a long way off, and he ran out to kiss him. He put a robe and a ring on him and threw this huge party to celebrate his boy's home-coming. That father is the picture of God waiting for you, Janie. Not with condemnation, but with longing and deep love."

For the first time, Janie seemed speechless. Her eyes lit on his for a moment, then darted off, pensive. "If that was true . . . if I could have a love like that . . ."

"You do, Janie," Sam said. "All you have to do is reach out and embrace your waiting Father."

Her eyes blurred with tears, and she wiped them away as they fell.

6

It was midafternoon by the time Sam got back home, still shaking after his time with Janie. Kate, who got off at three, would be home soon unless her ride didn't bring her straight here. He saw that the light on his answering machine was flickering, so he pushed the button and dropped down on his couch while he listened.

"Hey, Sam, it's me—Bill. Me and the guys'll pick you up at six for the game. Jeff and Steve are coming, but Brother John can't come because he has a meeting tonight. Call me if there's a problem."

Sam sat up quickly. He had completely forgotten about the game he had tickets for tonight. It was the biggest game of the year, between the two biggest state universities. They went every year, but this year was particularly exciting because neither team had lost a game yet.

But then he realized that this wouldn't be like other years. *He* was different.

What would it be like sitting in those stands and hearing all those needy souls around him? He thought of begging off.

He lay down on the couch and tried to take a nap, catch up on some of the sleep he'd lost the night before, but those voices he'd heard today kept circling through his mind. The woman who thought gravity would let her go; the one who thought she was her past; the man who thought he was dirty . . .

He sat up and thought of the people in the houses around him, all of them with voices and needs. What if he could address them all? Help them as he'd helped Janie? He realized this "gift" was going to hound him. But even Christ took time to rest, he thought. Then he berated himself. He had spoken to a few people about Christ today, and now he was patting himself on the back, thinking he deserved a nap. As if he'd addressed multitudes, cast out demons, healed the sick . . .

What was the matter with him? He could do better than he'd done. He didn't have to cower away in his house for fear of hearing what he didn't want to hear. He should see this gift as John saw it— he should look at these as opportunities. He heard the kitchen door shut, and Kate shouted out, "Sam?"

"In here," he called.

She came to the living room doorway, still wearing her nurse's uniform. *She helps people every day,* he thought. *Maybe God should have given* her *the gift.* She would have done a better job of using it. She probably would have never considered using those lottery numbers. "What are you doing home so early?" she asked.

He lay back down on the couch and patted the cushion next to his hip. "Come here," he said.

She approached him slowly. "Are you all right?"

He shook his head. "Sit down." She sat slowly down beside him and touched his forehead. "You're not hot. Are you sick?"

"Sort of. Well, not really." He swallowed and looked up at her. "Remember that dream last night? The one I told you about?"

She nodded. "Vaguely. You were trying to catch a plane . . ."

"No, that was your dream. Mine was the coin. The voice."

"Oh, yeah."

"It did something to me. I mean . . . God did something to me."

"What?"

"He gave me ears . . . to hear. I mean . . . like he hears." Kate's expression reflected her confusion, and Sam sat up, putting his face close to hers. "I know it sounds crazy, but, Kate, you've got to believe me. Call John. He knows. I heard his soul, and then—"

"His soul?" she cut in.

"Yes. And other people's. Everybody I got near today. I heard their spiritual needs. What Christ hears. And John went with me, and we talked to people . . ."

"Went with you where?" She wasn't following him at all.

"To the diner and the hospital."

"You were at the hospital today? My hospital?"

"Yes. But I didn't look you up, because I was a little freaked out, and I didn't know what to tell you about it. But, Kate, we told people about Jesus. Or John did. I just kind of sat there like dead weight. What else is new? But then . . . Janie, the waitress. She accepted Christ today after I talked to her, Kate. And there was this pregnant woman with a little girl and Mrs. Beautral's husband. Did you know she had a husband?"

She was looking at him, as if mentally fitting him for a straitjacket. "No."

"Well, she does, and he had gallbladder surgery, and now he's a Christian."

"Because of his gall bladder surgery?"

"No, because of our visit. Kate, you're not listening!"

She got up and backed away. "Sam, you're scaring me."

"I'm scaring *me*," he said, sitting up. "Kate, I was in the grocery store, and I heard all these voices at the same time. But their mouths weren't moving. I was hearing their souls. Just what the Holy Spirit hears."

"Now I know this is a fantasy," she cut in. "You haven't been to the grocery store in years."

"I went to buy Tylenol. Kate, I'm telling you, I hear things people don't even know they're feeling."

She turned and headed for the kitchen. "I'm getting the thermometer."

"Kate!" He followed her into the kitchen, and as she rummaged through a drawer looking for it, he heard her voice.

"I wish I could have a broken heart again."

"Aha!" he shouted. "You just said you wished you could have a broken heart. I heard you!" His face twisted as he realized the words made no sense. "Why do you want a broken heart?"

She stopped riffling through the drawer and looked up at him. "I didn't say anything about a broken heart."

"You did!" he said. "You did say it. You said, and I quote, 'I wish I could have a broken heart again.'"

Dumbfounded, she closed the drawer and moved across the island from him. "When you say you heard that, what do you mean?"

"In your voice," he said. "I heard it, Kate. It must be in there somewhere, in your soul, even if you don't know it. Even if you wouldn't say it out loud."

Her eyes changed, and her mouth rounded in surprise. "It is."

"See? I told you. What . . . what do you mean, you want a broken heart?"

She seemed to struggle for words that she'd never uttered before. "I've been feeling like . . . like I'm not sensitive to the Holy Spirit anymore. Like I've gotten jaded. Like my zeal has faded. I keep thinking that I need God to break my heart so I can get back in tune with him. You know, 'Blessed are the poor in spirit.' Blessed are those who mourn.' I haven't mourned for Christ in a very long time."

"Yes!" he shouted, jumping. Startled, she backed farther away and grabbed a spatula, as if that would protect her. "Honey, I know just how you feel!"

"And you heard that?" she asked, obviously terrified. "In my voice?"

"I thought it was a curse," he said as tears came to his eyes. He crossed the room and, ignoring the spatula, took her shoulders. "Until I introduced Janie to Christ. And then I came home wiped out, like I'd just recited the Sermon on the Mount to five thousand people. I told *one person* how to know Jesus and I think I'm Elijah."

The shock was beginning to fade, and she looked fully at him now. "You really led someone to Christ?"

"Yes! Can you believe it? *Me!*"

"I've never done that," she said.

"Go with me tonight," he said. "to the game. The guys are picking me up at six, but I'll call them and tell them I'll just meet them there. John isn't using his ticket, so we'll run by and get his, and you can use it."

"You want me at the game?" She touched his forehead again. "You *never* take me to the game. It's guys' night out."

"I want you to come and see. I'll hear the voices. You can help me. Maybe I'll be less of a wimp when you're with me."

"But what'll you tell the guys? They'll think I made you bring me. They'll call you henpecked."

"I don't care what they think. I'll hear their needs too. Maybe I can light a fire under them to help me tell people. Think about it. We could spread out, all of us, and tell people about Jesus until the game's over. We could tell dozens of people about Jesus tonight. We could—"

She grabbed his wrist and began taking his pulse. "You're not going to tell them you hear voices, are you?"

"Well . . . I don't know. They're my best friends. My accountability partners. They can handle it."

"No, they can't," she said, dropping his wrist. "Trust me. You don't want to tell anybody else about this. Just . . . find another way."

"Fine. But will you come?"

"How can I refuse?" she asked. "I'm afraid to let you out of my sight. This could be the prelude to a stroke or something. Is your arm numb, Sam?"

"No," he said. "Kate, I feel great. Nothing is numb. I don't have fever or palpitations. I just have this gift."

She couldn't surrender her worries just yet. Those lines on her face were deep as she stared at him. "I'll come, but I reserve the right to have you committed after the game if I see fit."

He grinned and pulled her into a hug. "Fine. People there need Jesus too."

7

Sam and Kate showed up at the stadium just after kick-off. Sam pushed through the crowd of people and up to the section where he and his friends always sat. The three guys were already there, sitting side by side and yelling at the activity on the field. Sam led Kate down the row to the two empty seats.

"Hey, guys, how's it going?"

Bill looked up and slapped hands with him. "Kate, you decided to come out with Sam tonight?"

She gave him a contrite smile. "How will you guys ever forgive me?"

"Man, this is gonna give all of us a bad name," Jeff cut in. "When Andrea finds out that you got to come, next thing you'll know, we'll all have to bring our wives."

Sam glanced at Kate, hoping she wasn't offended. "You know, that wouldn't be the worst thing in the world."

"Look, I'll just go home . . ."

"Kidding," Jeff said. "I was kidding."

But Sam knew he wasn't. He squeezed Kate's hand as they took their seats. He looked down at the field, trying to figure out what was going on. Smathers had the ball and State had just made a first down. A cheer rose up around them, and his friends sprang to their feet.

Then he heard the voices.

"I need a miracle."

Sam looked around, trying to figure out where the voice had come from. It was someone to the left of him, but he couldn't zero in on it.

"I'm gonna die, right here. I'm gonna die and shrivel up."

This came from behind him, and he swung around. All the fans behind him were on their feet, yelling at the top of their lungs.

Next to him, he heard Bill's voice, cracked and high-pitched as he yelled at the referee for making a bad call. But there was another voice coming from Bill. A quieter one that seemed to whisper in Sam's ear. "I can't be used. I'm worthless."

He looked over at his friend, frowning. He couldn't believe that such a dismal thought could come from his soul while he stood on his feet, cheering and yelling at the game before them. Before he could react, he heard another voice from the row in front of him.

"Nothing makes any sense. It's all chance. Coincidence."

Then came the voice of a woman. "I don't know where to go from here. I've forgotten my way home."

None of the faces that went with the voices seemed depressed or dismayed. The people seemed intent on the game, as if it was the one most important thing in their lives. He was amazed at the contrast with what he was hearing from deeper down.

Beginning to feel sick, he realized he was sweating. Kate looked over at him as he unbuttoned his collar.

"Honey, are you okay?" she asked.

He shook his head. "No, I'm not. The voices . . . they're every-where."

She stared up at him, concern etched on her face. His hands were shaking again. It was like in the grocery store, only worse. The voices were surrounding him, pursuing him. There was no escaping them.

"You want me to go get you something to drink? Or maybe an ambulance?"

"Drink, yes; ambulance, no. I'll come too." He got to his feet, and Jeff leaned around Bill.

"Where you going, man? You just got here."

"I've got a headache, and I—"

The words were like a voice-over, blocking out what Jeff was really saying. "What's the matter with me? Why can't I bear fruit?"

Sam met Jeff's eyes and wanted to answer the question, but he couldn't think. Sudden panic came over him—what would his friend think of his heart reading? Grabbing Kate's hand, he almost knocked someone down trying to get out of the row, then they walked down the stadium bleachers until they were in the corridor where the concession stands were. There weren't many people there since the game had just begun, so he found a vacant area and hurried to it and leaned back against the wall. Kate was beside him in an instant.

"Sam, something's wrong with you. You're sweating, and you're breathing like you've run a marathon! Are you having a heart attack?"

"No," he said. "It's the voices I told you about. I can hear them everywhere. It's torture."

She stared at him for a moment. Her eyes filled with tears.

She covered her mouth with both hands and turned away from him.

He pushed off from the wall and turned her around. "Kate, what's the matter? Why are you crying?"

"Because I don't want you to be crazy," she said in a high-pitched voice.

"I'm not crazy," he said. "Didn't I tell you what you were thinking before?"

"Yes, but . . . this is too weird, Sam. I don't know if I can handle this."

"That's just what I thought. But then I used it, and . . . I can do it again. You'll see. The people out there, they're hurting."

As if his words were further proof that he was nuts, she shook her head. "Those people are cheering at a ball game. Half of them are drunk. They're *not* hurting."

"They *are* hurting," he said. "I heard their pain. I have answers I can give them."

"All right," she said, trying to calm down. She wiped her eyes. "What are we gonna do? Pull them away from the game one by one and tell them what their deepest need is?"

"I don't know," he said. He looked at the few people milling around near the concession stand. "All I know is I'm not gonna accomplish anything standing here." He stepped toward the concession stand, and she followed tentatively. A couple of people were ordering popcorn and hot dogs.

Kate watched him with dread, but he knew her concern had more to do with his health and his mental state than it did with his spiritual gift. She still didn't get it.

"What am I gonna tell my wife?" The voice came from a big

man standing close to him. He was munching on popcorn as he waited for his drink order to be filled. "She'll leave me. I'll be alone. I don't know how to fix things."

The words were so personal, so haunting, Sam wished he could just pass out right there on the floor and forget he'd ever heard any of them, but he forced himself to step forward. "Excuse me, but . . . well . . . I have a sense . . . that there's something going on in your life."

The man shot him an annoyed look. "What do you mean?"

"I mean with your wife. You're wondering what you're going to tell her about something, and you're afraid she's going to leave you."

The man caught his breath and took a step back. Kate caught Sam's arm and squeezed, as if to tell him to cool it, that he was about to get decked. "Are you a detective?" the man asked. "Did she hire you?"

The question startled him. "No, nothing like that."

"Because if she did, you can tell her that she's wasting her time. She's not gonna catch me at anything. You got that?"

"Man, this isn't about catching you at something," Sam said. "I don't know what you're involved in. I don't know what's going on with your family. All I know is that you don't have to sit here and wonder what it's going to feel like to be alone."

The man's face twisted. The concession worker brought his drink, but the man didn't see him. "That'll be six bucks," he said, holding out his hand. The patron ignored him and kept staring at Sam.

"Turn it over to God," Sam said. "Believe in him and he'll . . . uh . . . he'll direct your paths." Sam vowed to brush up on his Bible as soon as he had the chance.

Finally, the man realized that the concession attendant was waiting for his money, and he reached into his pocket, got out six dollars, and slapped it on the table. Before getting his stuff, he turned his worried eyes back to Sam. "What has she seen? Have you been following me? Have you got pictures?"

Sam glanced at Kate. Her grip on his arm tightened. "No, nothing like that. I don't even know who you are."

The man gathered his food and turned away. "Look, I've got a game to watch."

"Sure," Sam said, "you go ahead. But remember what I said."

The man started walking faster and faster, until he disappeared around a corner.

Kate caught her breath. "Why did you do that?"

"Because I heard him," Sam said. "He said, 'What am I gonna tell my wife?' That she was gonna leave him and he would be left alone. That's his spiritual need right now. I was trying to address it."

"Well, that was pretty good," Kate said. "Only next time, you might want to pick a guy who isn't built like RoboCop. He could have smashed your face in." She let go of his arm and stared up at him. "I'm sorry, honey, but this is a little strange. People aren't going to accept having you just walk up to them out of the blue like that."

"But I was right. Didn't you see the look on his face?"

"Yes! That's why it was so weird." She lowered her voice as someone walked by. "Sam, do you really think God gave you this?"

"Where else would I get it? I'm not psychic. I'm telling you, this is real, and it works. Just watch. You can help me," he said. "You and I can both approach people, and you can soften what I say so I won't intimidate them."

She looked as if she was about to cry again. "Sam, you know I want to. But I don't think I can just walk up to someone and start talking like that."

"My emptiness is soul deep," he heard a voice behind him say.

Sam swung around and saw another guy at the concession stand, lurking in front of the candy window, as if that could fill him up.

"If I could turn inside out, I'd just disappear."

Sam's face twisted, and Kate stepped closer. "Did you hear something again?" she whispered.

"Yeah. That guy over there. He said his emptiness is soul deep."

She looked at him, her eyes softening. "That's sad."

"You got that right. Stay here. I'm gonna go talk to him."

Reluctantly, Kate turned to the counter as if trying to decide what to order. Sam got behind the man in the line. "How ya doing?" he asked. He reached out to shake his hand. "My name's Sam. Can I talk to you for a minute?"

"About what?" the guy asked.

"About your soul."

"Oh, brother." The guy rolled his eyes and waved him off as he started to walk away.

"The void is so big that if you turned inside out you'd disappear," Sam blurted.

The man stopped cold and turned slowly around. His mouth fell open, and he tipped his head suspiciously. "Who are you?"

Sam's heart raced. "I'm a friend," he said. "Someone, I think, the Lord sent to talk to you about that void."

The man behind the concession stand leaned over, trying to get the man's attention. "Excuse me. May I help you?"

The man glanced back. "Uh . . . no." He looked back at Sam, surprise in his eyes. "Where do you want to talk?" he asked.

"We could just step right over here," Sam said. "It's as good a place as any."

The man nodded and followed. Kate stayed back, across the corridor, watching with amazement on her face.

The first quarter of the game had almost ended by the time Sam led the man in prayer. He met Kate's eyes and saw that she was crying again. This time she wasn't looking at him as if he was some kind of mental case. She was obviously awestruck.

And so was Sam. The man had been hurting, and he needed to hear what Sam could tell him. He saw Sam as an instrument of divine intervention, and God was answering a prayer that he hadn't even realized he'd uttered.

The two exchanged business cards so Sam could check on him later, and as the man went back to his seat, Kate came over and reached up to hug him. "That was the most awesome thing I've ever seen."

Sam felt like he was light enough to lift off into the air. "It was pretty awesome, wasn't it? Man, if I'd known it felt this great to introduce somebody to Jesus, I'd have been doing it all along."

"There you are!" someone called.

Sam looked up and saw Jeff coming up the corridor. "Man, we were wondering what happened to you. The first quarter is over. Pratt just scored a touchdown. It was beautiful. You should have seen it."

"I just scored one of my own," Sam said.

Jeff frowned and looked down at Kate, then stepped closer. "What do you mean?"

"I mean I was just standing out here, and there was this guy here, and I started talking to him about Christ, and, Jeff . . . you're not gonna believe this, but the guy accepted him. I prayed with him and everything."

Jeff frowned. "You're kidding me."

"No, I'm not kidding. It happened. Kate saw the whole thing."

Jeff looked down at Kate, then back at Sam. "Man, John's sermon Sunday must have really gotten to you."

He wanted to say that it had gone right in one clogged-up ear and out the other until the Lord himself had spoken, but he just grinned. "You should try it," he said. "Everywhere you look there are people who need Christ. There are so many of them."

"Man, if I did that, atheism would probably soar to all-time highs." He leaned over the concession stand and ordered a drink.

Sam remembered what he'd heard from Jeff in the stands. "You think you can't be used."

Jeff turned back. "Well . . . yeah, I guess so. I mean, I've got a lot of stuff in my past. Even since I became a Christian, there are a few things that would mess up my credibility."

"What's that Jesus said? 'If thy right eye offends thee, cut it out?'"

Jeff grinned. "I've never heard you quote Scripture before."

Sam shrugged. "Man, I've been quoting Scripture all day. Most of it wrong, probably, but at least I'm trying. Did I get that one right?"

"Sounds right."

"All I know is that there aren't enough people out there who know about Jesus. Think how it would change their lives if they knew!"

Jeff was beginning to look uncomfortable. "I wouldn't even know where to begin."

"Just come with me," Sam said. "Hang around here for a minute. You'll see what Kate saw. It's awesome. I'll approach somebody and we can just start talking and . . ."

"Man," Jeff cut in, "I didn't pay forty bucks for this ticket so I could spend the game back here."

Sam tried to hide his disappointment. "Okay, that's fine. We can try it later."

"Fine," Jeff said. He looked irritated as he paid for his drink, then turned back to Sam. "Are you coming back?"

"I don't know," Sam said. "It's a little noisy, and my ears are feeling kind of sensitive."

Jeff shot Kate a look. "Is he sick?"

"I don't think so, Jeff."

He took a sip of his drink and headed back up the stairs. Kate looked up at Sam. "You know, maybe he's not really a Christian. Maybe he just knows *about* Jesus. Maybe he doesn't realize it isn't the same thing as knowing him."

Sam shook his head. "No, I heard his need—it was about bearing fruit. He wouldn't have a need like that if he wasn't a Christian. He just doesn't begin to know how to be used."

"Neither do I."

Sam looked down at her. "Just tell them what Jesus did for you. That's what John told me this morning. That's all it takes. It's not complicated."

"But I can't hear their needs," she said. "I don't have the edge you have."

"Yes, you do. I can tell you what I hear."

A woman walked up to get a straw, and his words trailed off as he heard her voice. "I can't trust anyone. No one can be counted on. I need someone to tell me what to do, but there isn't anyone."

"Talk to her," Sam said, lowering his voice to a whisper. "Go up to her and start a conversation."

Kate looked terrified. "I wouldn't know what to say. What did you hear?"

"She can't trust anyone; she needs someone to tell her what to do. Go on, Kate, talk to her."

"But Sam . . ."

"Kate, God is giving you an opportunity. You're not going to blow it, are you?"

"That's not fair," she said. "He gave you the opportunity, not me."

He shook his head. "No, I'm gonna go over there and talk to that guy in a minute. And if you can talk to her and I can talk to him, in a very short time, we might just lead two people to Christ."

Kate looked over at the woman. She was gathering her food on a tray and was turning to leave. "I can't do it!" she whispered. Sam looked down at her. "You can honestly know what she's feeling inside, that she's hurting, and not do anything about it? You're a nurse. If she were to drop from a heart attack, you'd bolt forward and do CPR. What is the difference?"

Kate watched as the woman walked over to the other counter to get ketchup. She shot Sam a look, took a deep breath, and moved toward her. "Excuse me!"

The woman turned around.

"Uh . . ." Kate had an expression on her face that said her mind had gone blank and she couldn't think of another word. "You . . .

you look like you have your hands full. I'd be glad to help if I could."

The woman gave her a suspicious look. "That's okay. I've got it. I'm not going far."

Kate glanced self-consciously back at Sam. He winked at her, then started toward the other guy at the counter.

"Look, I know this is weird," he heard her say. "But I just had this sense . . . that you need someone to talk to but you can't trust anyone, and well . . . I know you don't know me from Adam, but I'm a good listener and . . ."

Sam grinned as he reached the man.

"If only someone bigger was in control," the man was saying, "and I wasn't at the mercy of that tyrant I work for."

Sam reached for the straws on the table and accidentally knocked them over. The man squatted and started helping him pick them up. "I've been so clumsy today," Sam said. He extended his hand. "Sam Bennett."

And as they began a conversation, Sam told him who was really in control.

8

Sam didn't return to the stands until the game was almost over. His friends, who usually gave each other the benefit of the doubt no matter how bizarre one of them acted, each asked Kate privately if Sam was all right. They were good guys, all of them. The four of them, plus John, their pastor, had become close at a Promise Keepers rally three years earlier. After that, they'd formed an accountability group that met once a week in Bill's office. They prayed for each other diligently and held each other mildly accountable for their Christian walk. But it occurred to Sam as they pushed through the crowd out into the parking lot that none of them had been very fruitful over the years. They'd stayed cloistered in their own little group and had done essentially nothing to reach out to people in need.

As they reached their cars, Kate turned back. "Look, I think I'll just go on home. I'm pretty whipped from working so hard today. Sam, can you ride home with one of the guys?"

Sam shot her a look and started to tell her not to go, but then he realized he needed this time to talk seriously with his friends.

"I'll take him home," Bill said.

"All right. I'll see you guys later." She reached up and pressed a kiss on Sam's lips, then whispered, "Be careful." He watched her as she got into the car, then he rejoined his friends. "So what's this about you standing in the corridor the whole game, leading people to Christ?" Bill asked as they headed to his car.

"Man, I know it sounds crazy, and you probably won't believe it. But I've just had the most incredible day. I took the day off today and spent it with John. We met all these people and visited in the hospital. He was telling people about Christ left and right, and I got in on the act. It was the most amazing thing."

Bill's eyes twinkled as he took in the story. "It sounds great, man, but do you really think somebody who prays a prayer in a football stadium really knows what they're getting into?"

Sam frowned. "What do you mean 'what they're getting into'?"

"Don't you think you're selling them an easy believe-ism? A repeat-after-me kind of faith?"

"That's not what I'm doing," Sam said. "They need Jesus Christ, and I'm trying to show them where they can find him."

"I'm sorry," Bill said. "I don't mean to be a wet blanket. I just think that sometimes when things come that easy, maybe they really haven't come at all." They reached his car and he unlocked the door. All the guys climbed in.

"All I know," Sam said, settling into the backseat next to Jeff, "is that we meet once a week and we talk about God and all the things he's doing in our lives, and we ask for prayer for each other, and we do devotionals, but how many of us have really influenced anyone else?"

They were all quiet as Bill pulled into the line of traffic waiting to leave the stadium. "There's a harvest out there, and God needs workers," Sam said.

"I just believe I can influence people with my life," Steve said, looking over his shoulder. "At work, people know I'm different. They tell me all the time, and then I'm able to share with them that God is the difference."

"How many times has that happened?" Sam asked, genuinely wondering. "I'm not criticizing, really. Just curious. How many times has someone come up and asked you what's different about you?"

Steve thought for a moment. "Well, last year, people commented on how I behaved when Joan had cancer. Several people mentioned it."

"And what did you tell them?" Sam asked.

"I told them I relied on my faith to get me through."

"Did you tell them about Jesus? Did you pray with them?"

"No, I didn't have to."

"Are those people Christians today?"

Steve was getting angry. "What are you trying to do, man? Pick a fight?"

Sam sighed. "No, nothing like that. I'm trying to point out to you how lame it is just to hope that somebody will figure it out by the look on our faces." The other two guys were acting peeved, too, so Sam backed off for a moment as Bill pulled into the Shoney's parking lot. They were quiet as they went in. Sam closed his eyes, wishing he couldn't hear the waitress's soul saying how powerless and worthless she was. He tried to block out the sound of the man he passed who thought no one cared about him, or the mother who thought life was too chaotic, or the girl whose fear was an overwhelming dread in her heart, or the old man who rued the fact that he could never make anything of himself. All the needs, all the fears, all the dread, all the emptiness. His eyes burned with emotion as he reached the table and sat down.

There are so many people in here, he thought. *I would never have time to go to them one by one and address their needs.* He needed helpers. He needed others to share the burden.

They sat down and the other three guys quietly began looking at the menu. "Look," Sam said. "Look around you at everyone in here. That girl over there, she's scared to death. Feels like life is just too big for her, pressing down on her and she can't breathe."

Bill glanced over at the girl. She didn't look hopeless at all. "What are you talking about?" he asked.

"And that old man over there," Sam said, "he thinks he'll never make anything of himself."

"Well, if he hasn't already," Jeff said, "then he probably never will."

"He can realize that God has already made him valuable by creating him in God's image, that he's special because somebody died for him. He can be a saint and a joint heir with Christ. We have that information. Why are we withholding it from him?"

"Withholding?" Steve asked. "Come on, Sam. You're being a little melodramatic."

"Somebody needs to tell him, Steve," Sam said. "And see that woman over there? She thinks nobody cares about her. She feels all alone. And the waitress who brought us to the table feels completely insignificant."

Steve looked at him with disgust. "How do you know these things?"

"I just know," Sam said. "Every single person in here has a spiritual need. Take you three for instance . . . you need to be fruitful and do the work that Christ started. But no, you don't do it. And so your need isn't being fulfilled. You're the one standing in your own way. Not the church, not your jobs, not anything. Just you."

Bill looked down at the menu, his jaw popping. Steve stared across the table at him, still disgusted. Next to him, Jeff began tapping his fingers. "Sam, we just wanted to go out and have a good time. Watch a ball game. Crack a few jokes. Why do you have to make this so heavy?"

"Because people are dying," Sam said. "There's a hell and it's real and people are going there. Someone in this room may not make it home tonight."

Bill slammed his hand down on the table. The patrons around them looked up. "Since when are you so worried about people's souls?" he whispered harshly.

"It should have happened when I became a Christian," Sam said. "But it actually didn't happen until this morning."

"So let me get this straight," Steve said. "You went out with John this morning and told a few people about Christ, and now you think you're the apostle Paul?"

"No, I don't think anything like that," he said. "I'm a Christian. Bottom line. That's it. That's all there is."

The waitress interrupted and took their orders, and Sam looked up at her, desperately wanting to tell her that she was valuable, that she was precious in the sight of her maker. But he was in the middle of making a point with his friends, and he couldn't decide which was more important.

She went around the table and took their orders for coffee and soft drinks. When the waitress had scurried away, he looked around at each of them. "Let's make a plan," he said. "Tomorrow night, we drop whatever we're doing, we go out to the mall or a Laundromat or the hospital, somewhere . . . and we start talking to people about Jesus."

They each looked at him as if he'd just suggested going for a swim in a sewer.

"I have a Boy Scout meeting with my son tomorrow night," Bill said. "I can't go with you."

He looked at Jeff. "What about you?"

Jeff shook his head. "No, I told Andrea I'd be home tomorrow night. After being out tonight and choir practice Wednesday night . . ."

"Bring her with you," Sam said. "She'll love it. She'll really get into it."

Jeff compressed his lips. "I said no, Sam. Not tomorrow."

Sam looked at Steve across the table. "Come on, Steve, you can come with me."

Steve shook his head. "I'm sorry. I'm just . . . not ready for that."

"Ready for that?" Sam asked. "What do you mean?"

"I mean, I'm not prepared. I don't know what to say to people. You know, I have considered taking that evangelism class John told us about Sunday, maybe learning a few verses of Scripture, practice a little, learn how to share my faith before I actually go out there and do it."

"Man, you don't need a script." Sam looked from one man to the next, crushed that he couldn't persuade them. "If you could just *hear* what's going on in people's hearts!"

Bill gaped at him. "Like you can?"

Sam wanted to tell them, but he knew they'd never believe it. "Bill, it's our job to go out and tell people."

Bill blew out a sigh, then looked at his watch. "It's getting late, and I'm tired."

Sam stiffened. "We didn't get our drinks yet."

"I know, but I'm getting a headache." Bill got to his feet. "Let's just go."

"Am I making you that uncomfortable?" Sam asked. "Man, I've looked you in the eye and questioned your parenting. I've challenged you about your prayer life. I've held you accountable for your language. You've never gotten hot at me before. Why now?"

Bill sat back down and rubbed his face. "I'm not mad, Sam. I just don't quite get where this is coming from."

"Maybe . . . God? Ya think?"

The other men kept their eyes riveted on his, and suddenly Sam realized he was going about this all wrong. He didn't need to shame them into talking about Jesus. What he needed to do was get them excited, fill them with stories about what had happened to him today. The joys and the victories. "Guys, just listen for a minute. I want to tell you about some of the people I talked to today. Just open your minds and listen."

The waitress came back with their drinks, and the four of them sat there as Sam went on and on about the pregnant woman with the little girl, and Janie, the waitress, and the man tonight who had wept and accepted Christ at the stadium. At last he ran out of stories, and they sat, uncomfortably quiet.

He wondered if he should give up. "I've really put a damper on the whole night, haven't I?"

"No, it's just late." Bill's voice was flat. "I'm tired. Need to get home."

"All right." He got up and followed them wearily to the car.

They got in one by one, none of them saying a word. Sam was the first one Bill took home. When they pulled into his driveway, Sam waited a moment before getting out. "Guys, I'm really sorry for coming on so strong tonight, but this is serious business." He hesitated, waited for some kind of response, but there was only silence. He opened the door. When it was clear that they were all waiting for him to get out, he did. "See you guys later," he said in a weak voice.

They muttered their good-byes, and he closed the door. He drew in a deep breath and let it out slowly as he walked to the front of his house. "Help them, Lord," he whispered before he went inside. "Work on them like you worked on me. Give them a chance to know this joy."

9

Kate was already in bed when Sam came in. He leaned down and kissed her cheek. She smiled and hugged him. "John called. Said he needs to talk to you, no matter how late."

"Good."

"How did it go with the guys?"

Sam began unbuttoning his shirt. "They may never speak to me again."

"Why not?"

"Because I made them uncomfortable." He sank down on the mattress next to her and slumped over with his elbows on his knees. "Oh, Kate. I was awful. I was sarcastic and accusing . . . No wonder I didn't make any headway with them."

"You should have just witnessed to someone else right there in front of them, like you did me. Let them overhear you telling someone about Jesus. That would have done it."

"Yeah," he said, regretting the missed opportunities. "There was a waitress in Shoney's who really had a deep need. I was too distracted with them, so I didn't talk to her."

"You can go back tomorrow."

"Yeah." He got up. "I'd better let you sleep. You have to get up early."

She turned over to go back to sleep, and Sam went into the living room, too revved up for bed. It was just after ten. He wondered if John was still awake. He was glad the pastor needed to talk. He could use an ear himself.

He dialed John's number.

"Hello?"

"John? It's me, Sam."

"Hey, Sam. I just wanted to touch base with you and see how things are going. Kate said you'd been turning the stadium upside down."

"Yeah," he said, as the joy began to return. "Man, you should've been there. Tonight at the ball game, I kept hearing the voices. It was driving me crazy, so I went to the concession area and started talking to people as they came by."

"All by yourself?" John chuckled. "This morning you were scared to death to talk to strangers."

"Yes," he said, "but you helped me through it. Then I got Kate involved and she started doing it."

John began to laugh, and Sam grinned. "What is it?"

"I don't know why I'm always so surprised when prayers are answered," John said.

"You prayed about this?"

"I pray for all of you, all the time. I pray and beg and plead with God to give us revival so our members will be bold about sharing their faith, and now this is happening. I feel like a teenaged boy who just got a new car or something. Do you realize what could happen to our church because of this? If other people start to catch your zeal, and people are led to Christ, and—"

"Well, don't get too excited," Sam cut in. "It doesn't seem to be working like that."

"What do you mean?"

"Well, tonight, I told Bill, Jeff, and Steve about all the people I'd talked to today and how I was feeling."

"Did you tell them about the voices?"

"No," he said. "I didn't think they could handle that. You gotta admit, that's like something out of the Twilight Zone. I just told them your sermon Sunday got to me and that I had started to feel an urgency."

"That's good," John said.

"And true. But the problem is, they weren't that interested. In fact, they're pretty steamed at me right now. All of them."

"Why?"

Sam shook his head. "I told them all about what I had come to understand today. I told them about the people we had visited and what had happened. They just sat there looking at me like I was crazy, like they were upset that I would have the gall to tell them about this."

"It challenged them," John said. "I can get away with it from the pulpit, but one on one, face to face, they don't like it very much."

"But I heard their needs, John. I heard what they feel. That they need to be used. It's something they want. The Holy Spirit in them is crying out to do something."

"But their flesh is so weak, they don't realize they want it," John said.

"They had all these excuses. Boy Scouts and time with their wives—which never kept them from doing anything before—and fear of saying the wrong thing. It was the most amazing thing I've ever seen."

"Doesn't surprise me," John said. "I deal with it every day. Ninety-nine percent of the congregation is just like them."

"What about this evangelism class you mentioned?" Sam asked. "Didn't it start yesterday?"

"Yeah." John sounded underwhelmed.

"Well, how did it go? Maybe I could call on some of them."

John was quiet as he seemed to consider that. "I had high hopes for that class," he said. "I thought the preparation would shoot through some of their excuses. I thought maybe I'd have a couple dozen people show up, but it didn't work out that way."

"How many did you have?"

"Just a handful. *Less* than a handful."

"Well, still. That's some. Maybe I could call them and they could go out with me tomorrow night."

"All right," John said. "I'll give you their names. They're people who really do want to be fruitful. Maybe they'll agree to go." By the time he got off the phone with John, Sam realized it was too late to call anyone else. He set his list by the phone for the next day, then fell into bed, exhausted, and thought about the dream that had plagued him the night before. He wondered if he would dream tonight. He wondered if, when he woke, that gift would still be there.

But the next morning, when he got up, he realized it was still there when he heard Kate's voice yearning for another person to lead to Christ today. Not able to make himself wait longer, he began to call down the list John had given him. The first person he reached told him he couldn't go out, that he was afraid and was hoping that the class itself would help him with the fear factor.

"Words don't come easy for me," the man said. "I just would feel better if you could wait a couple of weeks."

The next person said something similar. "I've already got plans tonight. Tickets to the musical. My wife would kill me if I backed out."

One by one, he went down the list of hopefuls, and though his call was met with a little more interest than he had seen the night before, he had the distinct impression that these people were terrified of doing what he had done yesterday. Was there no one in the church who would help him with this harvest? No one other than the preacher?

He took Kate to work and headed to the diner to get breakfast, wondering if Janie had changed her mind overnight or forgotten their talk yesterday. But as he walked in, he could see that something was different in her. She was beaming, and she looked rested. It was clear that Christ was still with her. The normal chaos in the diner seemed more settled today, and even the cook was quieter.

He took a place at the counter and waited to hear the voices that would bombard him as soon as anyone got near. Janie came rushing up to him the moment she spotted him. "Hi, Sam. Listen, I tried to call you last night, but you weren't home. I needed to ask you something."

"Sure, what?"

"My sister. I want to tell her what you told me yesterday, only I'm afraid I don't know what to say. I want her to know Jesus too, and I was wondering if you would come with me to talk to her. I mean, I'll do the talking, but I thought it might be better if you came along so that if she has questions, or if I do, you'll be there to answer them. There's nothing worse than me trying to explain something I don't completely understand myself."

He looked up at her, his eyes bright with emotion. "Janie, I would be honored."

"Can you do it tonight after you get off work? I told her I was gonna come about seven."

"Yes, I can come then."

"Then, if it's not too much trouble, I wondered if you would come with me to the restaurant where my son works as a waiter. He takes a break at nine o'clock, and I was really hoping that we could talk to him and some of his friends . . ."

Sam couldn't believe it. He'd spent all last night and this morning trying to find someone in his church to help him with the harvest, and already one of his fruits from yesterday was anxious to reproduce. Was this the way it was supposed to work? he thought. Maybe it was.

"I tell you what, if you don't think it'll be too many people, I'll bring Kate with me tonight too. Then if we need to split your son and his buddies up and talk to them one on one, there'll be more of us to go around."

Janie was almost dancing as she considered that. "Meet me here at six-thirty, and we'll head out," she said. "This is gonna be so much fun!"

10

Once again, Sam was earlier to work than most of the people in his building. His secretary wasn't in yet, but someone had made coffee. He poured himself a cup, then went into his office. He dug through the bottom drawer of his file cabinet and took out his Bible. An old church bulletin marked his place, but he couldn't remember the last time he'd read from it.

There was so much he needed to know, he thought. So much that still eluded him about Christ. People would ask. He needed to be prepared. He wished he'd memorized more Scripture. He wished he'd hidden it in his heart.

A new hunger to know the Word overwhelmed him, and he began to read, marking passages and writing in the margins, trying to commit verses to memory. He didn't notice as the employees began to fill the building and the work day officially began. So when someone knocked on his door, he was startled. He looked up and saw his boss, Rob Simpson, with one of his biggest advertising clients standing behind him.

"Sam, I thought you might like to know that Mr. Hagle is here." Sam got up and came around the desk, extending his hand. "Mr. Hagle, it's great to see you."

"Sorry I missed you yesterday," the man said. "I took Rob to lunch."

"I wasn't feeling well," Sam said. "Long story, but I'm better today."

The man glanced at Sam's desk. "What's that you're reading?"

"The Bible," Sam said. He looked at his clock and realized eight o'clock had come and gone. "Guess it's time to be putting that up."

He heard a voice coming from the client, though his lips only moved in small talk. "I wish there was something in there for me. Light at the end of my tunnel."

Sam seized the opportunity to pounce before he could lose his nerve. "You know, Mr. Hagle, I don't know if you've ever read the Bible. If you haven't, you ought to give it a try. It sure does add light to the end of a long, dark tunnel."

The man's face changed. Frowning, he locked eyes with Sam. "I'll keep that in mind."

Sam nodded. Rob hurried the client out of the room, and Sam stepped into the doorway and watched until they'd turned the corner. Sam went back to his desk, closed his Bible, and put it away. He began working on the account that was sitting on his desk, calling for his attention. After a few moments, the phone buzzed. He picked it up. "Sam Bennett."

"Sam, this is Rob. I want to see you in my office. Now."

Sam closed his eyes. Maybe he had made a mistake mentioning the Bible and his faith to a client. Was Rob about to chew him out? He hurried to his boss's office and knocked on the door. He heard a gruff, "Come in."

Slowly, he walked inside. "You wanted to see me?"

"Yeah, I wanted to see you," Rob said, leaning back in his chair. "I want to talk to you about what just happened."

"What did just happen?" Sam asked, taking the chair across from his desk.

"I bring a client by your office, and you're sitting there reading the Bible, of all things. And as if that isn't bad enough, you have the gall to start telling him that *he* needs to be reading it." Rob got to his feet and began pacing back and forth across the office. "How do you think that makes the company look? How much faith do you think that man's going to put in us, when he sees you soaking up a bunch of superstitious philosophies and telling him *he* needs to do it?"

Heat rushed to Sam's face. "Look, Rob, I didn't know you were coming to my office. I came in here early this morning and started reading. The time got away from me."

"You were reading it on our time," Rob said. "It wasn't your time—it was our time. You never know when a client's going to stop by. You can't let them catch you doing something so stupid—"

"It was not stupid," Sam said, springing to his feet. "That is God's Word, not some stupid, superstitious philosophy, as you refer to it." It was the first time he'd lost his temper with his boss, and he knew he was getting dangerously close to losing his job.

Then he heard the voice, coming from Rob's soul, deep within him, too loud to ignore. "I can't stand my life anymore."

The words stopped Sam cold.

"My tunnel's so dark and so long that it's already swallowed up all the light."

Sam's anger vanished, and he looked into his boss's eyes and felt a compassion that he hadn't felt before. "Rob, the light can't be swallowed up."

Rob shot him a disgusted look. "What are you talking about? What light?"

"The light at the end of the tunnel," he said. "The darkness is never gonna swallow the light, because it's God's light and it's there, in his Word."

"It's a book!" he yelled. "Just words on a piece of paper, and I don't want it in my company. I will not have it ruining the credibility that we have with our clients. Either you get that through your head or you pack up your office and get out of here."

Sam realized that his boss was hurting. Something was going on in his life, and since he couldn't read his thoughts, but only the general emptiness of his spirit, he didn't have a clue what it could be. He grabbed a pad from Rob's desk and began to write.

"What are you doing?" Rob demanded.

Sam tore the page off and handed it to Rob. "This is my home number. I want you to call me any time you want to talk. I mean any time, night or day. Two in the morning. I don't care."

"Why would I call you in the middle of the night?"

Sam shrugged. "I don't know. I get the feeling that you need to talk."

"I'm talking right now! I told you to pack up the Bible or pack up your things!"

"I know," he said, "but I'm serious. If you need to talk, call me. Or you could come to church Sunday. I go to Church of the Savior on Post Road. Come and hear more about . . ."

"Get out of my office!"

"All right, Rob. I'm sorry I got you riled up." Before Rob could respond, Sam headed back to his office and closed himself in. He went back to his desk. They could keep him from reading his Bible on company time, he thought, but they couldn't keep him from praying. Quietly, he began to pray for Rob and the spiritual need he'd heard in his soul. As he did, he had a sense of peace, that God was working on Rob just as he'd once worked on Sam.

11

For the rest of the week, Sam reveled in his gift. He began to look forward to hearing the voices of the souls in the places he went. He even sought out crowds so that he could have access to more and more people. Kate, too, caught the zeal and began to rush home after work so they could go out to eat and find people to talk to.

When Sally, his secretary, didn't win the lottery, she failed to come to work for several days. Concerned about her, he finally paid her a visit.

As he stood on her porch next to the plants that needed watering, waiting for her to answer, he hoped that his gift hadn't been responsible for her withdrawal. He never should have repeated those numbers back to her. If he hadn't, maybe she wouldn't have put so much hope in the numbers being God's gift.

The door squeaked open, and Sally peeked out. Her eyes were red and swollen. "Sam?"

"Sally, are you okay?" Sam asked.

She nodded and swiped at her nose with a tissue.

"Can I come in?" She hesitated for a moment, then reluctantly stepped back to let him in.

"I wasn't expecting company," she said, "now that I'm not a millionaire." She said the words as if she'd been robbed of her fortune and all her friends had fled.

"It's fine," he said, stepping over wadded tissues on the carpet. Boxes of items cluttered the floor—a computer, a new television, a stereo system. Sam looked around and wondered if she had charged them on her credit card, planning to pay them off when her lottery numbers were chosen. The room was dark, as if she had been sitting there, crying and staring at the things she had coveted.

"I had so many affirmations," she said in a hoarse, stopped-up voice as she dropped miserably onto her sofa. "You even repeated the numbers I had in my head. How could that be if they weren't the right numbers?"

Sam realized he had unintentionally led her down the wrong path. He had almost used his gift to go that way himself. "I didn't know the numbers, Sally," he said. "How could I know?"

"But you said them!"

"I just had this feeling . . . about your spiritual condition. That your self-worth was somehow tied up in this lottery. That maybe I was even one of the people you wanted to show your true worth to."

She grabbed another Kleenex and blew her nose. "If I had become a multimillionaire, we'd see who was superior then."

"Why do you want to be superior?"

"Because I'm tired of being inferior. Equal would have even been good. But now I'm still just a peon."

"You've never been a peon, Sally. I couldn't get any of my work done without you."

"You'd hire another secretary in ten minutes flat. I wouldn't even be a fond memory." She began to cry again on the last words and pressed the wadded tissue to her eyes.

"Sally, you don't seem to know how much you mean to God."

"God?" she asked. "What's this got to do with God?"

"God cares more about you than he does some lottery ticket."

"Obviously he cares *nothing* about my lottery ticket. Not a thing. *Less* than nothing!"

"But you're not listening. He cares about you. And he knows you're worth a whole lot more than money. You're worth everything he had to give—Jesus gave his life for you."

"Oh, don't give me that," she bit out. "I know all about the cross. I was raised in church. I'm there every time the doors open. I teach Sunday school. I take food to poor families at Thanksgiving. I know more than you do about Jesus!"

"But knowing about Jesus doesn't do you much good, Sally. The Bible says that you have to 'confess with your mouth that Jesus is Lord, and believe in your heart that God raised him from the dead, and you will be saved.' If you believe in your heart that God did that, Sally, then why can't you trust him with your finances? Why can't you believe that you're worth a lot more than money?"

"Well . . . I do believe that . . . I do."

But Sam could hear her soul, and he knew she didn't really believe it. Not in her heart. They were just words to her, words she'd heard over and over throughout her life. Words that had little meaning to her. In her heart, where it counted, she didn't really believe.

"I just . . . wanted to be rich. If God loved me so much, he would want me to be rich too."

"What makes you think that God's business is making his

people rich? Maybe he needs you to stay in the middle class for some higher purpose. Maybe he even needs you poor, so he can use you a certain way. His children have a much higher value than dollars and cents. He has a plan for you that's better than any winning lottery ticket."

She was getting angrier. "If you weren't my boss . . ."

"What? What if I weren't your boss?" Sam waited.

She threw her chin up. "If you weren't my boss, I'd grab you by the throat and throw you out of my house!"

"Why?" he asked.

"Because you've got a lot of nerve, preaching to me. I'm one of the pillars of my church. I don't need you coming in here telling me about Jesus in my time of grief."

Sam got up, his hands innocently outstretched. "I've offended you—I didn't mean to do that. I just thought you should know that Jesus cares about you."

"I do know. I guess you're gonna fire me now. Kick me while I'm down!"

"No, I'm not going to fire you," he said. "I'm going to pray for you. That you'll understand how precious you are to God."

"I'll show you," she said. "I'll show you all. I'll win that lottery next week. If I buy enough tickets, I'm sure to win one of these times. I'm not one to give up this easy!"

Sam left her house and got back into his car, feeling sick that he hadn't been able to do better than that. *This is hard*, he thought. He closed his eyes and dropped his forehead onto the steering wheel. "Lord, please help Sally. My coming to see her was not enough. You've got to draw her to you. I can't do any of this by myself. Without you there with me, my words are empty. Useless."

When he started his car and looked back up at her door, he had tears in his eyes. Humbled, he drove off, aware more than ever that this gift had its limitations.

But Sam didn't let his visit with Sally stop him and decided to depend more than ever on the Holy Spirit to lead him. He lost count of the number of people he led to Christ, as well as the number who rejected him outright. The more he told, the more he wanted to tell, and the greater the urgency in his soul grew.

He couldn't wait until Sunday so he could try to appeal to some of his Christian friends at church to get out there with him. He had been praying earnestly and diligently about it, as Kate had, and he had faith that the Lord would provide helpers for the harvest.

Sunday morning, he and Kate went to the Waffle House for breakfast and shared the gospel with an old man who was sitting there alone. It almost made them late for church, but they pulled into the parking lot just as the organ music began to play. Sam hurried into the foyer, then through the double doors into the sanctuary.

And he stopped cold. The church was packed. He realized he had never seen it this full since they'd completed the new building three years earlier, not even on Easter. They had built it hoping for church growth, but the numbers had declined since that time. Today, however, every pew was full, and folding chairs had been brought in at the back. Even the balconies had people in them.

He looked at Kate and saw that her eyes were glowing. Taking her hand, he slipped into a back pew as the congregation rose and began to sing. The pastor stood at the front of the room, beaming with excitement and joy. Sam looked around him as they sang.

There, across the room, he saw Janie, the waitress, with her sister who had accepted Christ a few days before. Down the row was her son with two of his friends.

Kate nudged him and he followed her gaze across the aisle. It was the woman she'd spoken with at the ball game the other night. Two rows in front of her was one of the people he'd met at a convenience store. His eyes scanned the crowd, and up toward the front he saw Sid Beautral, from the hospital, and his wife. The man looked weak, but his face was full of joy.

When the praise time ended, John began to preach the sermon that was so much like the previous Sunday's. But last Sunday no one had heard. He talked about Luke 15 again, about the lost coin and the lost sheep and the lost son—he said that they were all things that others might have shrugged off as insignificant, but Jesus saw them as important enough to stop everything to seek them. As John preached, Sam prayed silently that the other Christians in the room would hear and respond, that their hearts would be opened to their true potential—reaching a lost world.

"I'm going to do something different today," John said. "I can't help thinking that some of you here would like to profess God before men. We're going to have an altar call, and I want you to come if you feel convicted to share what Christ is doing in your life." This time, Sam didn't check his watch as he had the week before. Instead, he continued to pray, not caring if anyone saw his eyes closed.

Kate nudged him again, and he looked up. A crowd was forming at the front of the room as the people sang on. He strained his neck to see who had gone forward. He saw Janie and her sister and her son, the lady at the ball game, Sid Beautral, and countless others they had met that week.

His eyes began to fill, and he covered his mouth and began to weep. Kate was already crying as if her heart was broken, but he knew the joy that bubbled in her soul as she clung to him. As the music leader led them in another verse, he hoped they wouldn't end the altar call yet. There were others, he knew, more of them who needed to make commitments. They needed another verse. Another song. Another hour. He sang clear and loud, his voice reaching out a prayer of thanks and supplication to his Father.

And then he saw another man slip out of the aisle and head down to the front.

"Anyone you know?" Kate whispered.

He wiped the tears from his face and narrowed his eyes to see through the blur. As the man turned to the side to whisper to John, Sam realized who it was. "That's Rob. My boss."

Kate stood on her toes to see over the heads. As Rob began to weep, head to head with John, Sam had to restrain himself from leaping forward and running down the aisle himself. Then another came, and another, and at last, he realized that almost as many heard the gospel from Kate as from him or John. People began moving from the front pews to make room for those who had come down. It was a marvel he hadn't been prepared for.

When John was satisfied that no one else was going to come, he nodded to the minister of music and they closed the song. Finally, when the music had stopped, John went back to the pulpit with a tear-stained face.

"Brothers and sisters," he said in a voice full of emotion, "I want to introduce some people to you. They've each accepted

Christ this week, and the story is the same over and over. A handful of these I spoke with, but the rest of them were led to Christ and invited here by either Sam Bennett or his wife, Kate."

Sam hadn't expected to be mentioned, and as heads turned and people sought him out, he looked at the floor, unable to meet their eyes. He didn't want the recognition, he thought. He just wanted help from other Christians.

"Sam?" John said from the pulpit.

Sam looked up.

"Would you come up here for a minute, please?"

Sam had no idea what John wanted him to do, but he got up, wiped his face, and walked the aisle. He went up to the pulpit and stood next to John, his face wet with his tears.

"Something's happened to Sam this week," John said. "This past week, he started listening to people's needs. One by one, he and Kate led these people here today. But they need help. I want to ask you, those of you who want to be like Sam, who want to help change people's lives, come to my class today at 4:00. Let's learn some Scripture you can use when sharing your faith, talk about ways to seek out the people who need to hear. Let's figure out how we can tap into Christ's vine to make our own branches bear fruit. And please come up and welcome our new brothers and sisters."

Then, one by one, he began to introduce those who had come, welcoming them to the family of God, embracing each one of them. Sam was there to accept the hugs and thanks of all who had come. When Rob came up, Sam reached for his hand. Rob pulled him into a hug. "Thank you," he whispered, overcome.

"You didn't call," Sam said. "I haven't even seen you at work."

"I've been thinking about it all week," Rob said. "I couldn't stop thinking about what you'd said. You may have saved my life. I owe you, big time."

"No," Sam said. "It's not me you owe."

By the time everyone had been welcomed and greeted and most of the congregation had left the church, Sam was exhilarated. A handful of people lingered behind.

Lawrence Shipman, the chairman of the deacons, approached him with a concerned look on his face. "What are you doing to get these people into church?" he asked. "Bribing them? Offering them food? What?"

Sam hadn't expected a question like that. "I've been telling them about Jesus."

"I want to know what they expect," he demanded as if he hadn't heard Sam, "coming here and bringing all their friends like that. Do they think they're gonna get something out of it?"

"They'd be right if they think that," Sam said. "They are gonna get something out of it."

"But some of these people don't fit in with our congregation," Lawrence said. "Did you see how some of them were dressed? Like they'd come straight from a bar. Church may not be the place where they need to be."

Sam's face began to grow hot as it had with Rob in the office the other day. He opened his mouth to tell Lawrence that people with his attitude were the reason for the stagnant state of their church for the past few years. But before he could formulate the words, he heard the man's inner voice. "I'm powerless. I don't have any control."

Sam's anger vanished. "Lawrence, there isn't a person on the face of the earth who wouldn't be welcome in this sanctuary, as far as I'm concerned."

"We have to exercise some kind of decorum. These people can't just sluff in here wearing tennis shoes and torn up blue jeans and bleached hair with black roots. Look around. That's not how we look."

"No, we wear all our sins on the inside, don't we? Packed away nice and tight, in clean little packages."

The man looked as if Sam had just slapped him across the face.

"Lawrence, I know you feel kind of powerless right now, but we're not supposed to be in control. God is. It's his house, not ours."

"Powerless? This isn't about power!"

"Of course it is," Sam said. "There are people at this church who would rather die than give up their power to the Holy Spirit."

"John!" Lawrence raised his voice, summoning the pastor over. John turned from talking to two other deacons and joined them. "You can't just stand there and let this happen. They're gonna ruin our church and change the whole face of our congregation."

John grinned from ear to ear. "I should hope so, Lawrence. I've been trying to do that myself for a long time. It looks like the Holy Spirit has decided to answer my prayers."

Lawrence shook his head and muttered something about calling a deacons' meeting and bringing this before the outreach committee. Then with a red face, he stormed out of the sanctuary.

John's expression lost its joy as he watched the man leave. "What did you hear in that, Sam?"

Sam shook his head. "I don't think he's a Christian."

"He thinks he is, though," the pastor said. "The Pharisaical kind. Setting a bunch of rules, but forgetting the relationship."

Sam set his hand on John's shoulder. "Don't let him ruin it for you, John."

John's face slowly lit back up. "I won't. Sam, thank you for helping with the greatest Sunday I've ever had in the pulpit."

"I just did what you taught me and what the Holy Spirit gifted me to do."

"Then you'll be back this afternoon to visit with the class?"

"I sure will," John said. "And let's pray for some of them to help us out."

But that afternoon, there were only eight at the evangelism class, and they all still had reasons why they weren't ready to talk to others about Jesus just yet. Still, they couldn't help being inspired by the number of people who had come down that morning. One of them suggested that they plan a "Let Us Rejoice" party for Friday night and invite the whole church to celebrate with the new believers, as the angels in heaven rejoiced. John thought it was a wonderful idea and an excellent opportunity to baptize them.

"We'll have to have food, lots of food," John said. "Kate, would you mind heading that up?"

"Not at all," she said. "We may not be able to recruit people to witness, but they're always willing to make food."

Sam didn't have much to say about the party. His joy in introducing people to Jesus was at an all-time high. He didn't see a reason for celebrating when there were still so many people out there who didn't know Christ. So many needs. So many people hurting. Every moment he spent with people afraid to be obedient to the command to evangelize the world was a moment that he was taking from people who needed him. He couldn't wait for the meeting to end so he and Kate could head to the mall.

That night, they led eighteen people to Christ.

Friday night, Sam showed up at the "Let Us Rejoice" party and congratulated all those he'd led to Christ. Modestly, he accepted words of praise for his good work from congregates who'd had several days to think about what he had done. He cried through the baptisms, but when they were finished and the party began, Sam grew restless. There were places he had to go, he thought, people he had to see. Needs he had to hear. He told Kate he was going to slip away, then quickly, he disappeared.

It was the Luke 15 kind of thing, he thought. He had to tear the house up and find that coin. He had to leave the ninety-nine sheep and look for the one. He had to scan the horizon for that lost son.

Tonight, something told him there would be lost sons coming in from out of town.

He drove to the bus station, where he had refused to go with John a few days earlier, and timidly, he walked in. There wasn't a bus there, but several people in the lobby were waiting for one to arrive. He sat down on a bench next to a woman with a baby . . . and began to listen.

But instead of her voice, he heard the sound of his cell phone ringing. He had started carrying it in his pocket so that anyone he'd witnessed to who might have questions could get in touch with him night or day. Quickly, he pulled it out and answered.

"Sam, this is Bill. Where are you, man?"

He hesitated. Bill, who'd had little to do with him since the game, had been at the party when he'd left. "I'm at the bus station. Why?"

"Because I was just thinking," he said. "Looking around at all these people who look so happy and thinking that never in a million years could I have led any of them to Christ . . ." His voice cracked. "Look, man. The Lord's really been working on me since that game the other night, and I'm thinking that maybe I need to come and help you out."

Sam got slowly to his feet. "Really?"

"Yeah. You got enough to go around? Because Jeff and Steve are standing here with me, and they'd kind of like to come too."

Sam threw his head back and laughed out loud. This was too good to be true. "There's a bus due in twenty minutes," he said. "There'll be plenty for all of us."

"All right, stay put. We're on our way."

A tear rolled down Sam's face as he dropped his phone back into his pocket.

12

Kate was already home when Sam returned that night, and he came in and called out for her. She rushed into the room, her hands on her hips. "How many?" she asked with a grin.

He shrugged. "I can't even say. Some of them listened. Some didn't. But the main thing is that Bill and Jeff and Steve got initiated into the harvest."

"I know!" She clasped her hands and did a little dance. "I couldn't believe it when they told me where they were going. Did *they* have any success?"

"Each of them led at least two people. It was phenomenal. They were practically jumping up and down. You should have seen it. And then I gave Bill a ride home, and all the way he kept thinking of different people he was gonna tell tomorrow. I think it's gotten into his blood now. There's no turning back."

Kate squealed and threw her arms around him. "You know, I have never been so proud of you as I have these last two weeks."

"Well, I'm pretty proud of you too."

"Don't be. I haven't done nearly what you've done."

"Well, like you said the other day, I have an edge."

She sat down, and he told her about some of the people he'd met, their needs, the ways he'd answered them. They laughed and wept and prayed together.

Later, when she went to bed, Sam stayed up. He was too energized to sleep, and he wanted to spend some time with the Lord. Humbly, he got down on his knees and thanked God for the blessing of ears with which to hear, for the needs he was able to fulfill, for the heart of flesh that had replaced his own heart of stone. And then he thanked God for the soul-winners he was raising up among Sam's friends and his brothers and sisters in Christ, and among the babes in Christ who had new stories to tell and new circles of friends who needed to hear.

Then he sank down in his recliner, opened his Bible, and began studying the Scripture. There was so much he had to learn, he thought. His soul soaked up all he read, digesting everything he saw.

Hours later, he fell asleep with the Bible in his lap.

And again, he began to dream . . .

13

He dreamed of that lost coin, but this time he was the one searching his house, looking under things and on top of things. And then he heard that divine, powerful voice that he'd heard almost two weeks earlier. But the words were different.

"And lo, I am with you always, even unto the end of the age."

He jolted awake and realized he had fallen asleep in the recliner with his Bible in his lap. He felt as touched by God as he had that first night when he'd wakened in a cold sweat with his hands trembling and his heart pounding. Breathless, he got up and went into the bedroom. Kate was still asleep. He didn't want to wake her, because he didn't know what to say.

Finally, he stepped into the shower and let the water cool and calm him as it rained down on him. When he came out, Kate stirred and looked at the clock. It was 5:00 A.M. "Did you ever come to bed last night?" she asked in a groggy voice.

"No, I fell asleep in the chair," he said quietly. He pulled on his robe and sat down on the edge of the bed. "Kate, I had another dream. I heard God talking to me again."

Kate sat up in bed, her eyes squinted. "What did he say?"

"He said, 'And lo, I am with you always, even unto the end of the age.'"

"Well, that's a nice thought. Right out of the Bible. Jesus said it after he gave the Great Commission."

"Yeah, but why did I dream it?"

"Maybe to remind you of the Great Commission he gave you?"

Sam thought that over as he got dressed and headed early to the diner for breakfast. Since it was Saturday, he left Kate to go back to sleep.

Sam parked in front of the diner and went in. He scanned the patrons as he walked to the counter. Some of them were people he had talked to over the last two weeks. Some of them had prayed with him. Some had even come to his church and the "Let Us Rejoice" party the night before. They looked up at him and smiled, and he gave a cursory wave and went to his usual stool at the counter.

He sat down and glanced to his side, smiled and nodded at the elderly woman next to him.

Janie came up. "Hi, Sam. Ready for the usual?"

"Thanks, Janie."

As she scurried away to get his breakfast, it dawned on him that he hadn't heard any voices yet. He sat up straighter on his stool and swiveled around, looking one by one into the faces of the people closest to him. Normally, he would have heard three or four by now. But even the woman right next to him remained silent. He leaned closer to her and tried to listen. But nothing came. She was eating her bacon, nibbling on a piece of toast, and there weren't any words coming out of her heart or her mouth.

Janie came back and put the plate on the counter in front of him. He looked up into her eyes, frantically listening, trying to hear.

"What is it, Sam?" she asked.

He shook his head. "Something's different."

"What?"

"I don't know." He got up and started backing out. "Uh, look. I can't eat right now." He threw a five-dollar bill down on the counter. "Maybe I'll come back in a little bit."

She nodded with confusion, and he bolted out of the diner and onto the sidewalk. A group of Girl Scouts passed by with boxes of cookies. Out here, when people passed him, he used to hear souls crying out their deepest needs. Now he heard nothing except the sounds of car engines going by, an occasional horn, voices from people chattering as they passed. But not the needs. Not those deep needs that stirred his heart.

Almost frantic with the fear that the gift was gone, he went to his car and drove to the bus station. There he would be able to tell if he had really lost his gift, he thought. There, where needs ran rampant and people were in turmoil. In the middle of a crowd, he would be able to tell.

He got there just as a bus was pulling in to let people out. It had been driving all night, he supposed, and the people were tired. They looked rumpled and wrinkled as they disembarked. He bypassed the terminal and headed straight for the bus. One by one the passengers got off, and he tried to hear.

But there was nothing. The gift was gone.

Tears burst into his eyes, and suddenly, he felt helpless, insignificant. Useless.

He ran back to his car. Where he would go, he wasn't sure, but he had to do something, he thought. John, his pastor, came to mind as it had on that first day. If anyone could help him, John could. So Sam pulled out and headed to John's home.

14

John was sitting at his desk in his study, hunched over his Bible, when his wife let Sam in. Sam was as shaken as he'd been that first morning. He was drenched in sweat, breathing hard, and pushing trembling hands through his hair. "John, you've got to help me."

John looked alarmed. "Sam, are you okay?"

"It's gone!" he cried. "It's all gone!"

"What is?"

"The gift."

John got slowly to his feet. "How do you know?"

"I had another dream last night," Sam ranted. "When I woke up, I felt like something was different, and when I went to the diner, I couldn't hear the voices. I can't hear them anywhere, even at the bus station."

John's face went slack, and Sam realized how much of his hopes John had been pinning on Sam's gift. "Maybe it's just fading," John said. "Maybe it'll come back."

"No." Sam sat down and shook his head. "I just know that it's gone. I think I knew on some level when I woke up this morning. After that dream . . ."

John took the seat next to him and leaned forward with his elbows on his knees. "Tell me about that dream," he said. "Sam, what happened in this one?"

"It was about the lost coin again," he said. "This time it was *my* coin, and I was looking instead of just watching someone else look. And then God spoke to me."

"What did he say this time?"

Sam hadn't thought about it since he'd told Kate earlier. He closed his eyes and tried to remember. "He said, 'And lo, I am with you always, even unto the end of the age.'"

John sat back in his chair. "That's the last verse in the Gospel of Matthew. The last words Matthew recorded before Jesus ascended."

"Why would he say that to me?" Sam asked. "What does it mean?"

"Just what it says, I'd imagine." He stared at Sam for a long moment. "Sam, are you sure it's gone?"

"Gone," he said. "I've tried. I can't hear a thing. Just normal voices. Just what you hear."

He saw that John was struggling to hide the disappointment on his face. "I had kind of counted on it staying. I mean, I don't know what I was thinking," John said. "Guess I was exploiting you in some ways."

"That was fine," Sam said. "After I got a taste of it, I *wanted* to be exploited. God gave me the gift for a reason."

John walked wearily back around his desk and dropped into his chair. "I really don't know what to think, Sam. Sometimes when I'm at a loss, the best thing to do is pray. Let's pray."

Sam gratefully hunched over, and as they began to pray, he felt a sadness fall over him. He knew with a certainty that the gift would not return. The Lord had given it, and he had taken it away. When they'd said "amen," John looked up at him, thoughts passing like shadows through his own eyes.

"Maybe the gift was just for a season, Sam. Let's not look at the removal of it as something to grieve about. Let's remember the joy while you had it. Maybe it was just to give you a glimpse of the urgency of the harvest."

"Maybe so," Sam said. "But it doesn't make it any easier." His mouth twisted as he tried not to cry, and he covered his face. "I was getting used to winning people to Christ. The confidence I had when I could just walk up to someone and know what their needs were. Hear inside them, just like the Lord does. What am I gonna do now?"

"You don't have to quit," John said. "You can still tell people about Jesus, just the way I do, and everybody else you taught does."

"No," Sam said. "I can't do it without that gift."

John got up, came closer, and touched Sam's shoulder. "Go home and pray some more about this," he said. "Ask the Lord to show you what to do. He will. That's what his words were about, Sam. He hasn't left you. He's going to be right there with you."

But as Sam headed back out to his car, he felt very much alone.

15

Sam didn't make any stops on the way home. He pulled into the garage and quickly closed the door behind him, as if it could keep him from having to encounter anyone whose needs he couldn't hear. He went into the house and saw that Kate was up and dressed. She smiled hopefully at him.

"Where ya been?"

"I just went to the diner to eat," he said.

She grinned. "How many?"

Tears sprang to his eyes, and he shook his head and headed toward the living room where he dropped into his recliner. Kate followed, the smile on her face fading. "What's the matter, Sam?"

"It's gone," he said. "I can't do it anymore."

"Do what?"

"I can't hear," he said. "The gift is all gone. I went everywhere. I went to the diner; I went out on the street; I went to the bus station. I can't hear it anymore!"

Kate stood there a moment, dumbfounded. Then, frowning, she asked, "Didn't you say you had a dream last night?"

"Yes," he said. "It must have been God's way of telling me it was over."

"Wow." She sank down onto the couch. "So . . . what are you gonna do?"

"Nothing. What *can* I do? I'm useless."

She thought about that for a moment, then stood back up. "Wait a minute. *I'm* not useless, and I haven't been able to hear anybody's spiritual needs."

"That's true," he said, "but you knew what I could hear. We were a team—I gave you information. But I can't do it anymore."

"No," she said. "That was true of the first few, but after that I got a little more confident. You weren't involved in every single one. Some of them I talked to without you."

"But let's face it," he said. "We both had this false sense of security that I could read their thoughts and know what they were feeling."

The telephone rang, and Kate stared at Sam for a moment, obviously processing his words. He could see that she was going to protest again, but instead, she picked up the phone. "Hello? Yeah, he's here. Just a minute." She held the phone out to Sam. "It's Steve."

"I don't want to talk to him. I'm too strung out here."

"He already knows you're here," she whispered.

Sighing heavily, Sam grabbed the phone. "Hello."

"Sam, it's Steve. Listen, Joan and I went to the mall this morning, and there was this old man who'd been sitting on a bench all by himself, and I finally got up the nerve to approach him and start a conversation, and you're not gonna believe what happened."

"What?"

"He accepted Christ. He's gonna come to church in the morning."

Sam closed his eyes and smiled faintly. "That's good, Steve. That's great."

"And I was just wondering, if you're not doing anything, why don't you come on over here? I'm gonna be here for a while. There are people everywhere. I thought you and I could—"

"No," Sam cut in. "I can't."

"Oh." Steve sounded a little surprised. "Well, okay, that's fine, if you have another commitment."

Sam shook his head. "Not another commitment, Steve. It's not that. It's just that—" He glanced up at Kate. Their eyes locked. He knew she was waiting to see what he was going to tell him. "It's just that I'm not feeling very well. I kind of have a . . . an ear problem."

"That doesn't sound good. Well, don't worry about it, then. I'll just work on my courage. You know, I'm counting on having a 'Let Us Rejoice' party every Friday night."

Sam frowned. He couldn't see it happening. Not now, not without his gift. Things had changed.

"I'll just call Bill and Jeff and see if they want to come. They had a blast last night. It was like they suddenly discovered a talent they didn't know they had. Listen, you take care, okay? Hope you're feeling better by tomorrow."

Sam hung up the phone and stared at it for a moment.

"Steve asked you to go with him to tell people about Jesus, and you turned him down?"

"Kate, didn't you hear me? It's over!"

The doorbell rang, and Kate headed for it. Moments later, John was in the doorway. "He lost the gift," Kate was telling him, and John was nodding.

"I know. He came by the house and told me this morning."

Sam began to rub his temples, but John came farther into the room and sat down opposite him. "You won't believe this."

"Tell me," Sam said, not very enthusiastically.

John leaned his elbows on his knees. "I've been getting calls this morning from some of the people in the evangelism class. The party last night got them all excited, and they're starting to feel more confident. They want to go out and talk to people after class tomorrow afternoon. Bill and Steve and Jeff told me to sign them up last night. I just wanted to let you know. I thought that might cheer you up, since you started all this."

Sam shrugged. "I appreciate that. I guess the gift did a lot of good while it lasted."

"But it didn't do you any good, did it?" Kate asked.

Irritated, Sam looked up at his wife. "What is that supposed to mean?"

"You're just gonna quit, like you can't mention the name Jesus without some supernatural gift. But none of the rest of us have it, and we can do it. There's still a harvest, Sam."

"Hey, you didn't go out until I taught you how. Until I could feed you their thoughts."

"Well, I've done it *without* knowing their thoughts," she said. "I can do it again. I have the courage. Do you?"

John looked as if he'd gotten caught in the middle of a family squabble. Defeated, Sam sank back in his chair and said, "What do you want from me, John?"

"I just wanted to see if you would come to the class tomorrow. Go out with us. Help them get started."

"Why me?"

"Because God touched you, Sam. He had a reason. He blessed

you with revelations that the rest of us haven't had. You know things. And people respect you because you've succeeded."

"Then how come I feel like a failure?"

"Because you're not looking at it with God's eyes."

Sam stayed home from church the next morning, and Kate went alone. He didn't have the energy or the desire to go. But when she got back from church and told him that thirty-six people had professed Christ that day, he began to feel guilty for his attitude. "I'm going to the class this afternoon," Kate said. "I wish you would go with me."

He hadn't enjoyed spending Sunday morning in a dark living room, while his wife was worshiping without him. He knew he was being selfish. His brooding was only making him feel worse and was keeping him from the people who mattered most to him. "All right," he said. "I'll go with you. But I'm only doing it to show you that this is not going to work."

"It will work," Kate said. "That gift taught you how to care about people. And I don't think your compassion will disappear just because your radar isn't picking up their thoughts anymore." Her gaze softened as she touched his shoulders and looked into his eyes. "Tell me your compassion isn't gone, Sam. I liked being married to someone who cared."

Sam wanted to tell her that he was still that person, but he wasn't sure he was. Would his zeal cool to a lukewarm level as it had been before? Would his heart grow hard again?

He turned away. Behind him, he heard her heavy sigh. "It's up to you, Sam. You had a two-week crash course in being like Jesus. Are you gonna throw that back in God's face?"

A million answers shot through Sam's mind, but he wasn't

sure of any of them. He turned around and stared helplessly at her.

"I know how crushed you must be," she said softly. "I'm kind of crushed myself. But God has his reasons, Sam. You have to trust him."

"John wants me to keep being some kind of leader . . . to tell others how to win souls . . . to act like I know something they don't know. But I *don't*. Not anymore."

Kate's eyes brimmed with tears. "Sam, don't you care about the lost coin anymore? Doesn't it matter to you?"

Sam couldn't take the sting of her words. He went to the kitchen and grabbed his keys off of the counter. "I've got to think," he said. "I need to be alone. I'll just . . . meet you at the class."

"Will you really be there?" she asked, sounding as if she didn't carry much hope that he really would. "Do you promise?"

He hesitated for a long moment, searching her face for the answers he couldn't find within himself. "I promise."

Then, before she could probe deeper, he hurried to the car.

Sam drove around town for several hours, thinking and praying about the things that had happened to him. For the life of him, he couldn't understand the Lord's playing such a cruel trick on him. Why would he have thrust an unwanted gift on him, then taught him to cherish it, only to take it away? It didn't make sense.

He pulled up next to a park where children played, and he began to walk the path that wound through the trees. He found a bench in the shade and sat down as joggers ran by, their sneakers thudding on the concrete. On the playground just beyond the running path, children laughed and squealed, and dogs barked.

There was so much to hear, yet so little. It was all superficial now. He might as well be deaf.

He checked his watch and saw that it was time to head to the church. He had promised Kate, and he didn't like to break promises. He wondered if the class members would be able to see right through him. Wouldn't they know that something inside him had been snatched away? That he didn't have the "insights" anymore?

I want to hear like you do, Lord. I want to know what you know.

But as he ambled back to his car, he felt the hopeless, sick feeling that he would never come close to hearing like that again.

16

Sam was stunned when he walked into the classroom that afternoon and saw the number of people who had come to learn how to share their faith. He looked around and guessed that there were at least a hundred people there. Some baby Christians, some who'd been believers for years. Bill and Steve were bringing in extra chairs, and Sam joined in. At least he could do that, he thought.

When John finally got the class quiet, he searched the room. "Sam, would you come up here for a minute, please?"

Sam shot John a look that told him he was going too far. He set down the chairs he was carrying and moved to the front of the room.

"Sam, everybody here knows the success rate you've had in telling people about Christ," John said. "It's inspired all of us. Now, you can see from the size of this class, the fruit that it's borne. And I wanted you to stand up here for a minute and tell people what your secret is."

Shocked, Sam gaped at his pastor. Why would John humiliate him like this? What did he expect him to say? That he'd had a supernatural gift of hearing peoples' souls? John stepped closer and lowered his voice. "Sam, tell them what to do. Tell them how to listen. Tell them what to see. You know."

Sam's eyes filled with tears, and his mouth trembled as he shifted from one foot to the other. He met Kate's hopeful eyes, and she nodded for him to answer. He cleared his throat and tried to speak. His voice cracked as it came out. "Well, basically, the bottom line, I guess, is . . ." He cleared it again. "Well, uh . . . you just . . . listen. Listen to them talk. Look at their faces. Look in their eyes. Touch them. Use your common sense." Yes, he thought. That was exactly what he had done every time he'd had any success. Something inside him stirred, and he took a step toward the class.

"If you could just hear with the ears of God, for a day, or a week, or two weeks . . ." He wiped the tears before they could run down his face. "If you could hear what God hears, you'd never forget it." He stopped and took a deep breath and met Kate's eyes, then John's. "There's not a soul out there who doesn't have those spiritual needs. You've got to learn to look for them."

Someone in the back of the room raised her hand, and he nodded for her to speak. "Sam, what would you say is their most common spiritual need?"

He shrugged and thought the question over for a long moment, juggling the different answers that came to him, trying to decide what the most common and most important ones were. "Well, they need to know that they're loved, that there's hope, that there's healing, that someone's in control, that they're not a product of their past, that they can be forgiven, that they can be useful, that they're made in the image of God . . ." He paused and racked his brain for more.

But suddenly it came to him. There really was only one answer that filled those needs he'd been naming. The answer he'd been offering for the past two weeks.

He stood there for a moment as the thought took hold of him.

"You know, really," he said, "I guess the answer to all their ques-tions, the fulfillment of all of their needs, is Jesus Christ."

They were hanging on every word, and he looked around at them as the thought sank deeper. "Really," he said. "Anybody you walked up to, if you were to ask them what their deepest need was, and if they were to be perfectly honest, if they even knew . . . their answer would be Jesus Christ."

He glanced awkwardly at the pastor and saw that John was grinning.

Encouraged, Sam went on, "So what we need to do is go out there with the knowledge that we have information they don't have. We can tell them how to fulfill those needs. We can turn their lives around. They all have the same need, and that need is Jesus Christ."

"What if they already know Jesus?" someone else asked. "What would their need be then?"

Sam looked from his wife to his friends, to the people he had led to Christ. And then he knew.

I want a broken heart.

I need to be used.

I've wasted all those years.

He covered his mouth as those tears erupted again. Finally, he managed to speak, "The bottom-line, basic need of every real Christian," he said, "is to bear fruit like Christ. You can count on it. Every true Christian has that need, whether they want to admit it or not. The Holy Spirit in them, it just yearns for that. And the fur-ther they are from fulfilling it, the emptier they are. Jesus cares about filling that emptiness . . . for a lot of reasons. One of them is our own happiness, but the bigger reason is that . . . it's not about us. It's about advancing God's kingdom. *We're* about advancing God's kingdom. And if we aren't acting like Christ, then we're missing it. It's like we're children of the king, but we're living in a dirt shack and eating pig food."

He saw in their faces that they all understood. He saw the glow of excitement in their eyes, the tears of resolve and commitment.

"Once you start behaving like Christ, in every area of your life, it's like moving into the castle," Sam said. "You know you don't deserve that joy, but it's still yours. You are who you are. You have power and the inheritance and all the joy that comes with it. And once you feel that joy . . ." His voice broke off, and he looked down at his feet and struggled to rein in his emotions. "Once you have it, you'll never want to be without it again."

After the class, John suggested that they all go out somewhere and practice sharing their faith before their zeal started to fade. Sam felt that fear he'd had in the beginning, the first day he'd realized he had the gift. But as the people began getting their bags and coats and heading for the church vans, he realized that he had to do better than this. He couldn't be a coward. He knew more than they knew. He had been enlightened. And tonight, the truth had come from his very own lips. The further he was from being like Christ, the more unhappy he would be. He knew it firsthand. How could he go back now?

John patted him on the back as they left the room. "So where do you think we ought to go?" he asked.

Sam thought for a moment. "Let's go to the bus station," he said. "There's a bus due in about ten minutes. And those people need the Lord."

17

Needing to be alone, Sam took his own car and followed behind the vans to the station. As he drove, he felt a sinking feeling in the pit of his stomach. What would they say when they saw what a failure he was? Would they all quit? Would they laugh at him?

The vans parked, and his church friends began filing out just as a bus pulled up. He sat in his car for a moment as the weary travelers began to get off the bus. His eyes burned with fear, and his heart pounded. As he got out, he breathed a silent prayer, a prayer for courage, a prayer for confidence, a prayer that he could hear as the Holy Spirit heard.

The group of them broke up, and each approached someone and struck up a conversation. Sam stood with his hands in his pockets and listened as he heard various ones around the room explaining Christ in the best way they knew how. He saw an older man standing near the glass doors, looking out as if waiting for someone to pick him up. But no one ever came. Sam looked around, helplessly wondering whom—he should approach, what he should say to them when he couldn't confidently know what their needs were. Then he remembered the theory he'd come to in the classroom a little earlier . . . that every lost soul's need was the same.

Deciding to approach the man under that premise, he went to the door. "Hey, there," he said as he reached him. "How ya doing?"

The man nodded and smiled weakly.

"My name's Sam Bennett," he said, reaching out to shake his hand. "You waiting for somebody?"

"I thought I was," the rumpled old man said. "I thought my daughter was coming to get me, but—" His eyes reddened with emotion, and he looked away. "We don't get along so well and . . . I didn't really know if she'd come or not."

Sam's heart began to melt, and he realized that he was hearing the need. He looked through the glass door in the direction where the man had been looking. "Maybe she'll still come," he said. "Maybe she's just late."

The old man's mouth trembled as he shook his head. "No, I don't think she's gonna come. See, it's been a long time since I've been in touch with her, and well . . . I guess I crossed over the point where there's no goin' back."

Sam met his eyes and remembered the lost things of Luke 15. The lost coin . . . the lost sheep . . . the lost son. The poignancy of those stories assaulted him anew, and he realized that the Holy Spirit had reminded him so that he could tell the man. "There's never a point where you've gone too far," he said.

The man breathed in a heavy, soul-deep sigh. "Oh, yeah there is. And I crossed it a long time ago." Sam looked out the door again, wishing the daughter would come to show the man that there was such a thing as forgiveness and new life. But even if she didn't, there was someone else who would. There was a father, scanning the horizon for the sight of that lost son. "Why don't you let me give you a ride?" Sam asked. "I have my car out here."

"Weren't you waiting for somebody else?"

Sam shrugged. "Sort of. But they didn't show up either." The man looked at Sam with new eyes, as if he could understand how it felt to be rejected. "Come on. I'll take you to wherever you need to go."

"Well, I appreciate that, sir," the man said. "Don't you need to tell your friends?"

Sam looked over toward Kate. She was watching him and smiling. He winked and nodded that he was leaving. "It's okay," he said. "They've got another way home."

As he got into the car with the old man and asked where he wanted to go, he realized that the needs were right there on the surface . . . in the man's face . . . in his stance . . . in the way he carried himself . . . in his words. And what he couldn't hear, the Holy Spirit could. He could do what Sam couldn't.

This man needed Jesus Christ.

That was all he needed to know.

WHAT IF *YOU* COULD HEAR AS GOD HEARS?

Everyone has problems. Everyone has pain. But what would you do if you actually knew the spiritual needs of everyone you met? This is the compelling question asked in The Heart Reader of Franklin High.

Change A Life. Share Your Faith.

A moving, evangelistic challenge for all believers from an anonymous, best-selling CBA author. All royalties will be donated to Samaritan's Purse, a nonprofit Christian mission organization.